THE RESILIENT YOUNG ATHLETE

A PRACTICAL GUIDE TO DEVELOPING MENTAL TOUGHNESS, SELF CONFIDENCE, AND A GROWTH MINDSET AMID THE SUCCESS AND SETBACKS OF YOUTH SPORTS

CAROL ROBINS

© **Copyright Carol Robins 2024 - All rights reserved.**

The content within this book may not be reproduced, duplicated or transmitted without direct written permission from the author or the publisher.

Under no circumstances will any blame or legal responsibility be held against the publisher, or author, for any damages, reparation, or monetary loss due to the information contained within this book. Either directly or indirectly. You are responsible for your own choices, actions, and results.

Legal Notice:

This book is copyright protected. This book is only for personal use. You cannot amend, distribute, sell, use, quote or paraphrase any part of the content within this book, without the consent of the author or publisher.

Disclaimer Notice:

Please note the information contained within this document has been gathered to provide general advice and is not a substitute for personalized, professional advice. All effort has been expended to present accurate, up-to-date, and reliable, complete information. No warranties of any kind are declared or implied.

By reading this document, the reader agrees that under no circumstances is the author responsible for any injury, losses, direct or indirect, which are incurred as a result of applying the information contained within this document, including, but not limited to, — errors, omissions, or inaccuracies.

The content within this book has been derived from various sources. Readers should be aware that the application of techniques discussed within this document may vary based on individual skill levels, physical ability, and may not be appropriate for everyone. It is strongly recommended that readers consult with a professional coach, or other appropriately qualified sports or health practitioners before attempting any practices outlined in this book.

CONTENTS

Go Time!	7
1. THE FOUNDATION OF MENTAL TOUGHNESS	11
The Psychology of a Winner: Mindset Matters	11
Growth Mindset: The Key to Continuous Improvement	14
Parent's Corner: Growth Mindset	17
Overcoming Fear of Failure	18
Setting Learning Goals	19
Stay Curious, Stay Passionate!	21
Parent's Corner: Curiosity	21
Identifying Your Inner Strengths and Weaknesses	22
The Science Behind Stress and Performance	23
Stress Management Techniques	25
Cultivating Resilience: Lessons From Elite Athletes	27
Building Resilience	30
Parent's Corner: Resilience	31
Chapter One: Three Key Points I Need to Work On	33
2. DEVELOPING YOUR MENTAL GAME PLAN	35
How to Set SMART Goals	36
Short & Long Term Goals	40
Process vs. Performance vs. Outcome Goals	42
Monitoring Progress	43
Overcoming Mental Blocks and Barriers	43
The Role of Mental Preparation	46
Visualization	48
Parent's Corner: Visualization	53
The Power of Routine	54
Chapter Two: Three Key Points I Need to Work On	56
3. TECHNIQUES FOR EVERYDAY TRAINING	57
The Power of Positive Self-Talk	58
Four Types of Self-Talk	61
Journaling	63
Harnessing the Benefits of Mindfulness and Meditation	65
Meditation Techniques	68
Breathing Exercises to Control Anxiety and Stress	69

Four Breathing Techniques for Young Athletes   70
  Establishing a Consistent Training Mindset   72
  Chapter Three: Three Key Points I Need to Work On   73

4. **APPLYING MENTAL TOUGHNESS ON GAME DAY**   75
  Pregame Preparation: Getting Your Mind in the Zone   75
  Pre-performance Routines   77
  Effective Team Communication   79
  Staying Calm and Collected During High-Pressure Moments   81
  Managing Mistakes and Moving Forward   84
  The Power of Perspective   86
  The Art of Comebacks: Turning the Game Around   87
  Rafael Nadal's Stunning Comeback – 2022 Australian Open Grand Final   90
  Celebrating Success and Learning From Loss   91
  Chapter Four: Three Key Points I Need to Work On   93

5. **OVERCOMING FEARS AND ANXIETY**   95
  Strategies to Overcome Fear and Anxiety   96
  External Pressures   100
  Strategies to Deal With External Pressure   101
  Building Confidence After a Setback   102
  Steps to Recovery   103
  Parent's Corner: Learning From Setbacks   104
  Coming Back From an Injury   104
  Parent's Corner: Injuries   106
  Chapter Five: Three Key Points I Need to Work On   107

  Case Study One: From the Sidelines to Center Court - Ruben Borg's Story   109

6. **HANDLING CRITICISM AND FEEDBACK**   119
  Constructive Criticism vs. Negative Feedback   120
  How to Handle Negative Feedback   121
  Stephen Curry's Superpower   122
  Debriefing   124
  Coaches Corner: Debriefing   125
  Difficult Conversations With Coaches and Teammates   127
  Chapter Six: Three Key Points I Need to Work On   128

  Case Study Two: Local Talent to International Success - Kai Calderbank-Park's Journey   129

7. COACHES, TEAMMATES & MENTAL TOUGHNESS — 141
Team Culture — 142
Building Positive Coach-Athlete Relationships — 144
Three Famous Sports Partnerships — 145
Learning From the Greats — 148
Coaches Corner: Building Positive Coach-Athlete Relationships — 150
The Importance of Mentorship in Athlete Development — 151
You and Your Teammates — 153
Coach's Corner: Team Cohesion — 154
Navigating Competitive Friendships: Healthy Rivalries — 156
Rafa and Roger: The Ultimate Competitive Friendship Role Models — 158
Chapter Seven: Three Key Points I Need to Work On — 160

8. INVOLVING FAMILY — 161
Communicating with Your Parents — 162
Parent's Corner: Communication and Support — 164
Siblings — 167
Balancing Sports and Social Life: A Family Affair — 169
Chapter Eight: Three Key Points I Need to Work On — 171

Full Time — 173
After The Game — 177
Bibliography — 179

WORKBOOK

Useful Resource

The Resilient Young Athlete is filled with practical components to guide you on your journey towards sporting success. However, if you would like to explore these practical elements in greater detail, *The Resilient Young Athlete Workbook* serves as a valuable companion to your reading. This workbook provides additional exercises and content that offers a place to record goals, journal entries, performance analysis, plus much more all in one place!

If you would like to purchase this workbook please scan the QR Code below or search "The Resilient Young Athlete Workbook" in Amazon.

Amazon.com

Amazon.com.au

GO TIME!

Your heart pounds in your chest.

Beads of sweat trickle down your forehead.

Every fiber in your body screams with uncertainty as you face your opponent.

Yet, you should have this. You've trained for it so long that your reactions have become automatic. On the practice field, you've been dominating the competition.

But now, with the weight of expectation bearing down, you're starting to lose focus. The pressure of the moment threatens to overwhelm you. All your hard work—those countless mornings of getting up early and staying late—means nothing if you can't keep it together.

Its times like these where your mind can become your enemy, and doubt starts to gnaw at your insides.

I promise you, you're not alone.

For the past 16 years I have worked with immensely talented youth athletes and seen it time and time again....young people with incredible skill and ability, developed through years of training hour after hour, but who struggle with the pressure of competition.

So, what's the missing ingredient?

Mental toughness.

For young athletes, it's the difference between surrendering to defeat and rising above the pressure of the moment to let their skills shine. It's the silent force that separates the strong from the weak. Without it, all the natural talent, skill, and determination in the world mean nothing. But with it, you become an unstoppable force.

This book is your mental toughness manual. By you, I mean athletes between the ages of 13 to 18. My goal in writing it is simple:

> *To equip you with the tools and mentality needed to build confidence, deal with setbacks, and create the growth mindset you need to conquer in the world of competitive sports.*

Throughout these pages, you'll find real-life case studies and examples of professional athletes who have overcome mental barriers to become champions. There are also plenty of interactive elements, such as practical exercises, visualization techniques, and reflection prompts to encourage active participation and personal application.

Each chapter includes helpful advice and strategies covering the essential elements of mental toughness for young athletes. These include:

- Developing a Growth Mindset
- Setting SMART Goals
- The Power of Positive Self-Talk

- Getting Your Mind Into the Zone
- The Art of the Comeback
- Overcoming Fears and Anxiety
- Handling Criticism and Feedback
- Working With Coaches and Teammates
- The Importance of Family

And don't worry about any heavy reading. I've designed this book to be educational and inspiring. You'll find the content engaging and accessible, with practical tips and strategies you can apply immediately.

But this book isn't just for young athletes. It's for parents and coaches too. It provides the guidance often missing for these VIP's when it comes to helping young athletes win the mental side of sports competition.

As a parent, you'll discover strategies to support your child's athletic journey and learn ways to promote open communication, navigate difficult conversations, and deal with setbacks.

Coaches and mentors will also find strategies to actively contribute to the development of mental toughness through supportive practices and resilience building exercises.

Whether you're a young athlete, a parent, or a coach, I invite you to embrace the opportunities within this book's pages. The concepts and strategies you'll discover are the same techniques I've seen successful athletes adopt throughout my career as a sports scientist and coach to build resilience, confidence, and improve performance.

The journey toward mental toughness starts now.

Are you ready to rise to the occasion?

ONE
THE FOUNDATION OF MENTAL TOUGHNESS

THE PSYCHOLOGY OF A WINNER: MINDSET MATTERS

What makes a winner? Is it something physical, like muscular strength, speed, and agility? Or is it something inside you, like mental toughness and the ability to bounce back?

Time after time, we see proof that what you think about in the heat of the moment and how you respond can be more important than your physical ability. Consider the following:

During the 2006 FIFA World Cup final, soccer superstar Zinedine Zidane famously headbutted Italian defender Marco Materazzi in the chest. This earned Zidane a red card, and he was sent off for the rest of the game. The incident occurred during extra time, with Zidane's French team ultimately losing to Italy. When asked why he did it, Zidane said that Materazzi had insulted his mother and this had caused him to lash out in anger.

Nick Kyrgios is an Australian professional tennis player. He has a fantastic game but is often criticized for his inability to maintain composure and execute under pressure. He's been known to make unforced errors, argue with umpires, and lose focus when the stakes are high.

These examples highlight something every young athlete must take to heart if they want to succeed:

Being a winner isn't just about your skills; it's about having the right mindset.

In other words, it's not just about what you can do physically, but also how you think and feel inside.

To succeed at your chosen sport, you need to develop a winner's mindset.

So, what is it?

Below are the attributes that contribute to a winner's mindset:

- **Belief in Yourself:** Winners have unwavering self belief. They know they can achieve amazing things with hard work and dedication. This confidence remains steadfast, even when faced with criticism or the pressure of competition kicks in.
- **A Positive Attitude:** Winners stayed focused on the positives. They look for the silver lining in any given situation, and seek out solutions and opportunities for growth instead of dwelling on negative outcomes or circumstances.
- **Resilience:** Resilience involves being able to bounce back from challenges. It requires having the mentality to not let mistakes throw you off your game. It allows you to learn from setbacks to become stronger and wiser.
- **Perseverance:** Winners never give up, even when things get super tough. They know that every step, no matter how small, brings them closer to success.
- **Focus:** Winners stay focused on their goals and whatever the immediate task at hand requires. They have the ability to tune

out distractions like the crowd and concentrate on what they need to do in any given moment.
- **Adaptability:** Winners understand that things don't always go according to plan. They have the ability to reset, and can adjust their strategy to find new ways to win.
- **Gratitude:** Winners show appreciation for what they have and respect the people in their lives who support them. They show kindness and express gratitude to those who help them succeed.

If you can develop this powerful mindset, you will set the stage for overcoming challenges and achieving success in sports.

However, if you can't, you will likely waste many of your hard-earned skills. You may choke during a critical moment of competition, lose it when your game strategy isn't working out, or let self-doubt rob you of the skills you've perfected in practice when you need them the most.

Perhaps you've already experienced that frustration. After spending countless hours training, getting up early when you'd rather stay in bed, or maybe practicing late while your friends are out having fun... you still struggle when it counts.

Don't you think it's time for that frustration to end?

By developing a winner's mindset you will gift yourself the mental toughness you need to overcome the thoughts that prevent you from showing the world what you can really do.

Read that sentence again—it's very powerful!

The self-belief that comes with a winning mindset will help you stay positive and put things into perspective, even when things get tough. It will feed your motivation to keep getting better. Think of it like your inner coach, cheering you on and helping you stay focused. It will help you see setbacks as stepping stones to success. With it, you can bounce back when you stumble and keep training when you'd rather be doing a million other things.

A winning mindset also involves staying curious, setting goals, and finding joy in what you do day to day. When you love your sport, staying motivated becomes easy because you're driven by passion and a love for the process, not just by the pursuit of winning trophies, medals or gaining other accolades.

GROWTH MINDSET: THE KEY TO CONTINUOUS IMPROVEMENT

Think about the subject you dislike most at school. Maybe it's math. Do you think you can become better at that subject? Or have you just thought, "I hate math, so I'll never get it!"

What about your social skills? Have you told yourself that you're not good with crowds and never will be? Do you feel you are better off on your own, or in one-to-one situations?

How about when your teacher asks you a question that's a bit too hard for you? Do you think, "I'm just not smart enough for this?"

You show signs of a fixed mindset if you've answered yes to any of those questions. A person with a fixed mindset believes that their abilities are pretty much set in stone. You can make slight improvements, but if you struggle with math when you're 13, you'll still struggle with it when you're 30.

A growth mindset, however, is the opposite. A person with this mentality believes that their potential to develop in all areas is unlimited. All it needs is discipline and hard work.

For this reason, a person with a growth mindset is far more likely to achieve their goals.

Whether you believe you can grow and improve (have a growth mindset), or you think you're stuck the way you are and have a fixed mindset, may not be apparent to others. But it plays a significant role in how you approach challenges. If you have a fixed mindset, you might feel like you can't change your body or abilities, so you might not even try.

And even if you do try, that belief might secretly hold you back. It could make you cheat on your healthy eating plan, skip workouts, or tell yourself you'll never reach your goals.

The above has been emphasized in some really interesting research on kids with a fixed vs. growth mindset. In one study, children who were identified as having a fixed mindset were asked what they'd do next time after failing a test. Most of them said they'd cheat instead of studying harder.

In another study, children with a fixed mindset said they would find someone else who did worse on the test than they did so they wouldn't feel so bad. In most of these cases, the fixed-mindset students avoided difficulties rather than trying to get better and learn from their mistakes.

So, what about the growth-mindset kids? In every study, they took up the challenge. After failing a test, they said they'd study harder to get better results next time. They weren't afraid to acknowledge that they could improve and were open to learning.

Moving From a Fixed to a Growth Mindset

By now it should be clear that a winning mindset is a growth mindset. So, what if you've already identified you show signs of a fixed mindset? Well, the good news is that your fixed mindset is not fixed at all! You can change it.

Here are 10 things you can do right now to move from a fixed to a growth mindset:

1. **Think of challenges as opportunities:** Stop hiding away from new challenges because you think you might fail. Instead, look for ways to push yourself to improve, knowing that you might not get it right the first time.
2. **Make learning more important than getting praise:** When you're more concerned about other people's approval, you miss out on opportunities to grow. That's because you are

scared of failing in front of them. So, you must discipline yourself to stop worrying about other people's opinions and focus on improving for your own benefit.

3. **Focus on the process instead of the end result:** Enjoy the learning process, understanding that the growth and skills you develop along the way are more valuable than any one achievement. When you focus on the journey it creates an environment for continuous improvement and resilience, which are essential for long-term success.
4. **Develop a sense of purpose:** Create long-term goals that give you something meaningful to aim for and a sense of direction with your training. Keep the end goal in mind and set yourself this target as you work through daily challenges and smaller milestones.
5. **Choose learning well over learning fast:** Be patient and willing to make mistakes when learning something new. Attention to detail and concentrated effort goes a long way when refining your skills.
6. **Understand that making mistakes doesn't make you a failure:** Instead, it means that you're on the right track; you're just not there yet.
7. **Learn from the mistakes of others:** When you see someone else make a mistake, mentally take note for when you are in a similar situation. Pretend it was you and ask yourself, "How can I do better?"
8. **Welcome constructive criticism:** See criticism as a teachable moment. Don't take it personally. It is meant to help you improve, so embrace it with humility.
9. **Every time you achieve a goal, set a new one:** Don't be content with where you're at. Always have a new target to focus on and work towards. Personal growth has no end, especially when you're an athlete!
10. **Remember, it takes time to succeed in anything worthwhile:** Nothing worth doing comes quickly and easily.

To master a new skill, ability, or task, you must work at it over time. Progress in your athletic journey might not always come in leaps and bounds, but remember that every small step forward adds up over time. Trust the process and stay patient.

To think about ...

Take a few minutes to consider your mindset. Is it a fixed or growth mindset? How do you know? If you've got a fixed mindset, choose three of the above suggestions and work on them over the next seven days.

PARENT'S CORNER: GROWTH MINDSET

Moms and dads play a vital role in helping their child develop a growth rather than a fixed mindset. American psychologist Carol Dweck originated the concept of fixed vs. growth mindsets in her ground breaking research. Here's how Carol defines it:

> *In a fixed mindset, students believe their basic abilities, intelligence, and talents are just fixed traits. They have a certain amount, and their goal is to look smart and never look dumb. In a growth mindset, students understand that their talents and abilities can be developed through effort, good teaching, and persistence. They don't necessarily think everyone's the same, or anyone can be Einstein, but they believe everyone can get smarter if they work at it.*

Carol has also identified three things that parents can do to promote a growth mindset in their children:

1. **Praise wisely:** That means praising your kids for their hard work, strategies, focus, and perseverance. This will help them

develop resilience and learn to seek out challenges. Understand that when you only celebrate talent or successful outcomes, you make your child vulnerable to a fear of failure as your praise is conditioned upon a positive end result or performance.
2. **Use the words "yet" and "not yet":** When your child has a setback, gets a wrong answer, or doesn't pull off a sports skill, talk to them in terms of not being able to do it quite *yet*. This instills the confidence that they're on a learning continuum and will help them to succeed if they keep going.
3. **Educate about how the brain responds to challenges:** In one study, students were taught that whenever they pushed beyond their comfort zone to learn something difficult, the neurons in their brains formed new connections and became more competent. The students who learned this lesson on how the brain adapts to challenges showed significant improvements in their grades. This research emphasizes the importance of understanding that the brain is malleable and that effort and perseverance can lead to increased intelligence and abilities.

OVERCOMING FEAR OF FAILURE

Fear of failure is one sign of a fixed mindset. It often prevents people from trying new things, extending their skills, or embracing challenges. Learning to overcome the fear of failure can open a whole new world of possibilities.

The following are proven strategies to help defeat the fear of failure:

1. **Change how you see failure:** Instead of viewing failure as all bad, think of it as a chance to learn, set new goals, and be a stepping stone toward success.
2. **Don't expect to be perfect:** Understand that nobody is perfect, and everyone makes mistakes sometimes. Instead of

aiming for perfection, focus on trying your best and improving little by little each day. With practice the likelihood of errors will become less and less.
3. **Learn from mistakes:** When you make a mistake, consider what went wrong and how you can improve upon it. Remember, mistakes can be invaluable clues that show you what you need to work on.
4. **Keep trying:** Don't give up if you fail at something the first time (or even a few times!). Persevere, and don't let setbacks stop you from reaching your goals.
5. **Try new things:** Be open to learning new skills. These could include new physical techniques or tactical plays. Give these things a try even if you're not sure you'll succeed. Taking risks is part of learning and growing.
6. **Believe in yourself:** Have confidence in your abilities and believe you can learn and improve over time. Self-belief is the foundation for your growth and achievement. When you believe in yourself, you are more likely to take on new challenges, and the fear of failing is replaced with the excitement of potential success.
7. **Celebrate your efforts:** Even if you don't succeed, be proud of yourself for trying your best. Celebrate your efforts and remember that every step forward is a step closer to your goals.

SETTING LEARNING GOALS

People with a growth mindset are goal-setters. They know they can always get better, no matter how good or poor they are at a skill. As a result, they constantly set new challenges for themselves.

For many people though, setting goals doesn't come very easily. In fact, most people struggle with it. What they think are goals can often be nothing more than vague ambitions.

In Chapter Two, we'll examine how to set SMART goals to achieve sporting success. For now though, let's discuss setting learning goals that promote a growth mindset and skill development.

Your learning goals need to be built off of the areas of your game that you along with your coach have identified as needing improvement. They should follow the SMART acronym of being:

- **Specific:** Instead of setting a vague goal like "improving my game," athletes should specify what aspect they want to develop, such as passing accuracy or defensive skills.
- **Measurable:** Goals should be measurable so progress can be tracked. For example, setting a goal to increase passing accuracy by a certain percentage, or reducing a sprint time by a specific number of seconds makes goals more measurable.
- **Attainable:** Goals should be challenging but realistic. Unrealistic goals can lead to frustration and demotivation.
- **Relevant:** Goals should be relevant to the athlete's overall development and performance objectives. They should fit in with their strengths, weaknesses, and long-term goals.
- **Time-Bound:** Goals should have a deadline. This helps athletes to stay focused and motivated. Breaking down long-term goals into smaller, manageable milestones with deadlines can also make them more achievable.

Here is an example of what a poor goal looks like and what an effective goal is based on the SMART formula:

- **Poor Goal:** "To get better at passing."
- **Effective Goal:** "To improve my passing skills by practicing for 20 minutes every day for the next month, aiming to reduce the number of accuracy errors by 50%."

STAY CURIOUS, STAY PASSIONATE!

Athletes who have a growth mindset tend to demonstrate a couple of standout qualities related to their sport: they are curious and have a deep passion for the game.

When you're genuinely curious and passionate about what you do, your drive to succeed will come from inside you. You will be motivated to explore and master new skills.

This mindset also makes you more receptive to learning from those around you. When you're curious, you'll want to absorb as much information from your coach as possible, recognizing its value in helping to elevate your performance. You'll observe your teammates, learning from their strengths and strategies that you can incorporate into your own game. Even your opponents become sources of learning; analyzing their techniques and tactics will not only help you work out ways to win, but also provide you with a broader understanding of your sport.

PARENT'S CORNER: CURIOSITY

Parents play a crucial role in nurturing curiosity and passion within their young athletes. Creating an environment that encourages exploration, creativity, and enjoyment will help your child feel supported in pursuing their interests and goals. You can actively participate in developing this curiosity by watching games together, discussing strategies, and encouraging them to experiment with new techniques during training. By showing genuine interest and enthusiasm, parents can ignite a similar passion in their children.

Through adopting a culture of curiosity and love for the game, you will help your child develop the mentality and skills needed to thrive both on and off the field.

IDENTIFYING YOUR INNER STRENGTHS AND WEAKNESSES

As a young athlete with a growth mindset, you want to identify your game related strengths and weaknesses. You aren't afraid to examine what you're struggling with because you know it's not an attack on you personally. You can put aside your emotions and take an objective look at your performance.

You can also identify the strengths and weaknesses in your mental game.

So, how do you do it?

Here are three methods to accurately assess your strengths and weaknesses, both mentally and physically:

Self-Reflection and Journaling: Take time after practices and competitions to reflect on your performance. Writing down your thoughts in a journal can help you identify your strengths and areas for improvement. Be honest with yourself and use this self-reflection as a tool for growth. This is something we will delve deeper into during Chapter Three.

Peer and Coach Feedback: Ask your coach, teammates, and trusted mentors for feedback on your performance. Be open to constructive criticism and use it as an opportunity to learn and grow. When they talk, don't try to justify what you did or didn't do—just listen and be willing to have an honest conversation on what you need to work on.

Video Analysis: Video footage is a powerful resource for identifying strengths and weaknesses in your performance. Here's how to effectively use video for analysis:

- Have yourself recorded during drills, practices, or games, focusing on specific skills or situations you want to analyze.
- When watching the video footage, have a clear purpose in mind. Look for patterns, trends, and areas where you both

excelled or struggled. Pay attention to details such as body positioning, timing, and skill execution.
- When analyzing areas that need improvement, look for technical flaws, tactical errors, or missed opportunities. Compare your performance to that of more experienced players or pro athletes to identify areas where you can elevate your game.
- Share the video footage with your coach, teammates, or trusted mentors for feedback. Ask specific questions about areas of concern or aspects of your performance that you want to improve.
- Set SMART goals for improvement. Focus on one or two areas at a time to avoid feeling overwhelmed.
- Continuously record and review your performances over time to track your progress.

Once you've identified areas for improvement, don't think of them as weaknesses, but rather as undeveloped strengths. See them as opportunities to strengthen your overall game. Each skill you develop adds another arrow to your bow.

Try not to only focus on your weaknesses either; recognize your strengths as well. However, instead of being content with these areas where you are excelling, strive to improve upon these aspects of your performance even further—set goals to develop your strengths and continue to push your potential to new heights.

The key to turning your weakness into a strength is consistency. Stay committed and zeroed in on your developmental goals. Embrace challenges and setbacks as part of the learning process, and remain patient and persistent as you work to improve.

THE SCIENCE BEHIND STRESS AND PERFORMANCE

Is your life stressful? As a student-athlete, you've got a lot on your plate: your schoolwork, individual training, team practice, the pressure of competition, parental and coach expectations, dealing with siblings, managing friendships, and finding time for hobbies and relaxation.

With all that to deal with, no one can blame you for feeling at least some level of stress.

Stress in itself is not a bad thing. It's a natural response to the challenges we face. But unless we know how to control our stress, it can eat away at us like rust on a prized possession. Your performance on the field and in the classroom could suffer, and you'll struggle to keep up with the demands of academics and athletics.

Uncontrolled stress can also make you feel physically sick. It can bring on headaches, muscle tension, and make you feel fatigued. Mentally, it can lead to anxiety, frustration, and burnout.

To manage stress, it's essential to first understand what it is and why we experience it.

You can think of stress like a roller coaster. Some parts can be scary and make you feel ill, but other parts are exciting and make you feel alive. These two elements of the rollercoaster are like the two types of stress that we call **eustress** and **distress**.

Eustress is a good kind of stress. It's that nervous, excited, and pumped feeling you get before competing. This type of stress can help you perform better, feeding your energy and focus.

Distress however, is the opposite. It's when you feel overwhelmed, anxious, or worried. Maybe you've got too much homework, or you're feeling pressure from your coach or parents.

This type of stress can make you feel tired, frazzled, and out of your depth.

The critical thing to remember is that not all stress is bad. By keeping distress to a minimum and learning to make the most of good stressors, you can ride the roller coaster of life with confidence, resilience, and a sense of adventure.

STRESS MANAGEMENT TECHNIQUES

If you're feeling overwhelmed here are seven things you can do to cope with day to day stressors:

1. **Deep breathing:** When you start feeling stressed, take a few deep breaths in through your nose. Hold each breath for a few seconds, and then slowly exhale out through your mouth. Think that with each breath out you are releasing stress from you body and allow your muscles to relax.
2. **Take breaks:** No matter how busy you are, you need time to rest both physically and mentally. Take short breaks while studying or training to listen to music, play with your pet, or just get some fresh air.
3. **Communicate:** Don't keep your stress bottled up inside you. Talk about what's troubling you with a friend, parent, coach, or other trusted person. Just sharing what's bothering you can help mentally lighten your load and offer you with potential solutions on how to manage what's on your mind.
4. **Get organized:** The more organized you are, the less overwhelmed you'll feel. Use a planner or to-do list to keep yourself organized and prioritize tasks. Break down large tasks into small, more manageable ones and tackle them one at a time.
5. **Don't think ahead:** If you think about everything you've got to do, you'll soon become overwhelmed. So, once you've organized your tasks, focus on what is immediately in front of you or of most importance. Once it's done, tick it off your list and move on to the next.
6. **Get plenty of sleep:** When you sleep, your body and mind rejuvenate themselves. You need 8–10 hours of quality sleep each night. To get it, establish a bedtime routine that includes keeping all technology out of the bedroom—yes, that includes your phone!

7. **Set boundaries:** You can't do it all and don't always have to say yes. Don't burn yourself out trying to please everyone. Learn to say no to things that will add unnecessary stress to your life or don't align with your goals.

On the day of competition, knowing how to control stress is equally important. A handy acronym covering seven key strategies is P.E.R.F.E.C.T.

P is for Positive Self-Talk: Repeat words or short sentences to yourself in the heat of competition. Simple phrases like "I've got this," or "Piece of cake" will keep you zoned in on the task at hand. Self-talk will also be a topic we will go into greater detail with during Chapter Three.

E is for **Embrace Adversity**: Rise to the challenge of competition; if you're behind on points or trailing an opponent in front of you, write your own underdog story and refuse to let doubts creep in as you claw your way back.

R is for **Reverse Engineer**: Recall a time when you executed a skill with total confidence and succeeded. What cues helped you then—was it a particular phrase, a piece of clothing, or a physical cue? Once you identify it, try using it again.

F is for **Focus on the Now**: Be in the moment, every moment of the game. Don't think about the scoreline, or if you will win or lose. Just concentrate on what you need to do in the next few seconds to succeed.

E is for **Energize**: Prior to competition, fuel up with the right carbohydrates and other nutrients to help maximize your performance. This includes drinking plenty of water to stay hydrated. By taking care of your nutrition, you'll keep your energy levels stable for optimum performance.

C is for **Chill Out**: Schedule time to relax and recover after competition. You need to recharge your body and mind, so find something that rejuvenates you and enjoy spending time doing it. This could be anything from hanging out with friends or engaging in a hobby that helps you relax.

T is for **Talk It Out**: Debrief with your coach after the game or event. Talk about how you dealt with the stress of competing and your physical performance. Their insight or advice can help provide the perspective you need to better manage any future performance stressors.

CULTIVATING RESILIENCE: LESSONS FROM ELITE ATHLETES

Resilience is the ability to bounce back from challenges or hardship. It helps you remain calm when things start to fall apart and double down when it seems like the whole world's against you. Resilient people find strength in adversity, emerging more robust and determined than ever.

When it comes to sports, resilience is all about pushing through challenges, setbacks, and failure without giving up. It's about staying focused and positive, even when you're behind.

The resilient athlete knows that failure is part of the journey to success. They use setbacks as learning opportunities. If they suffer an injury, they don't let it derail their dreams; instead, they focus on their recovery with determination and patience.

Every successful athlete possesses this quality and has undoubtedly battled through their own adversities. Consider the following two pro athletes who have demonstrated incredible resilience and overcome numerous challenges to become two of the most undeniable greats within their chosen sports.

Tom Brady's Test of Tenacity

Tom Brady's name is synonymous with success. He is the most decorated NFL player of all time, and has won seven Super Bowl titles. He is a five-time Super Bowl MVP, three-time NFL MVP, and two-time NFL offensive player of the year!

However, Tom's rise to the top was a slow burn. During high school, Tom was a dual-sport athlete, playing both baseball and football. Despite showing more promise and receiving draft offers as a baseballer, Tom's love for football ultimately led him to commit to the University of Michigan Wolverines.

During his first year at Michigan in 1995, he deferred or "redshirted" his college football career, meaning he did not receive any game time. In his second year, he was finally given a chance to show what he was capable of, and was substituted on late into a game against UCLA. However, the first ever pass of his college career was intercepted for a touchdown, and was the only one UCLA would make all game. This left both Wolverine fans and his college coaches underwhelmed by his performance and questioning his ability.

For the 1996 and 1997 seasons, Brady was forced to take a backseat at Michigan, with another future NFL quarterback receiving the starting honors. Disappointed and frustrated, Tom considered transferring. He however attributes a shift in his mindset to working with University of Michigan sports psychologist Greg Harden. At the time, Brady admits he had a "victim" mentality when things did not go his way. Harden made Tom realize he needed to "stop complaining and start doing." He worked on helping Tom concentrate on the things he could control and let go of the things he thought were holding him back. To this day, Brady credits Greg as being one of the most important and inspirational influences on his football career.

Now armed with the tools he needed to push on, Brady decided to stay at Michigan. He also managed to gain the starting quarterback position, however still found himself sharing the role with another up-and-coming quarterback for the rest of his college career.

For this reason, Tom was not considered a standout by many NFL teams heading into 2000 NFL draft. It took until the sixth round of selections before he was drafted by the New England Patriots and ended up being the 199th overall pick.

As a rookie for the Patriots in 2001, Tom did not make the starting lineup. However, fate intervened at the beginning of the 2002 season when Drew Bledsoe, the starting quarterback, suffered a serious injury. This unfortunate incident left Brady gaining the starting honors for the rest of the season. Then, as they say, the rest is history! That year the Patriots won their first ever Super Bowl title, and Tom was awarded his first Super Bowl MVP award.

Tom's story demonstrates that despite years of adversity, resilience can be built through perseverance, hunger, and the right mentality. His journey from being an underrated college footballer and draft pick, to becoming an NFL legend showcases how unwavering determination and a strong mindset can overcome even the most toughest challenges.

Cristiano Ronaldo's Unlikely Journey

Cristiano Ronaldo is one of the most famous and skilled football players on the planet. Yet his journey to greatness is an unlikely story.

Ronaldo was born and raised on the small island of Madeira, Portugal. His family didn't have much money, so his parents had to work long hours to make ends meet. He lived in a very modest home and shared a bedroom with his three older siblings. With his Dad being passionate about football, Ronaldo found his love and talent for the game at a very young age.

When he was 12, Ronaldo was spotted by a talent scout and invited to a three-day trial to play for Sporting Lisbon in the capital of Portugal. During those three days, he competed with much older boys but didn't let that phase him. He pushed himself to the limit, impressed the coaches, and ended up with a contract at the club.

However, this meant Ronaldo now lived away from home and his family in a big new city. He struggled at school, got into fights, and was eventually expelled for throwing a chair at a teacher. Then, at 15 years old, he was diagnosed with a heart condition called tachycardia (an abnormal heart rate), which could have ended his football career before it even started.

Instead, he made the decision to have laser heart surgery and was back into training three days later.

Ronaldo's resilience was again tested at 18 when he transferred to Manchester United. He wasn't used to the physicality of English football and struggled to fit in. The pressure to perform from fans and management was overwhelming. But, rather than crumbling, he focused on improving his skills. By working tirelessly on his weaknesses and building up his strength in the gym, he became a key player for United.

Over the years, Ronaldo has also had to endure the relentless comparison to Lionel Messi. This rivalry has become a hot topic of debate in modern football, with anyone who is a football fan having an opinion on who is the GOAT (Greatest Of All Time). Every statistic, from goals scored, matches played, and trophies won, has been analyzed against Messi's. Despite this, Ronaldo's unwavering self-belief, mental toughness, and relentless work ethic have allowed him to thrive under the spotlight.

Cristiano's career is trademarked by his flare on the football field but also by his ability to knuckle down and keep going despite setbacks, criticisms, and comparisons. From humble beginnings and suffering through injuries and personal tragedies, he has endured it all with grit and determination. His journey is a testament to the power of perseverance and a reminder that true champions emerge stronger and more determined with every trial they face.

BUILDING RESILIENCE

Building resilience is like muscle strengthening—it takes time, effort, and practice. Here are a number of strategies that will help you on the road to becoming a more resilient athlete:

1. **Regulate your emotions:** In sports, things don't always go your way. In the heat of the moment it can be tempting to let

your frustrations get the best of you. Alternatively, if you have had a moment of success like scoring a goal, it can be easy to get carried away with excitement. In both these situations it is important to remember that until the game is over, you still have a job to do. Stay level-headed, focus on aspects you can control, and concentrate on what your next actions need to be.

2. **Be open to constructive criticism:** Criticism can sometimes be hard to hear but try not to take it personally. When coaches, parents, or even teammates provide you with feedback, remember that it's an opportunity for growth. Accept it with grace and humility.
3. **Challenge yourself:** Whether practicing a skill you're already competent at, or learning something new, look for ways to continually challenge your ability. Working just outside your comfort zone is how you get better both physically and mentally as an athlete.
4. **Make one percent decisions:** This means making the conscious effort to do the little things that, over time, will make you a better athlete. It could be as simple as opting for a healthier meal instead of fast food after a game, ensuring you hit the end line with every sprint performed at training, or going to bed early the night before a competition. Set yourself standards and hold yourself accountable.
5. **Think long-term:** Don't give up at the first sign of difficulty. Adjust goals if needed and keep pushing forward. Remember that resilience is built through perseverance and determination.

PARENT'S CORNER: RESILIENCE

Parents have a crucial role to play in helping their children develop resilience. Seven key areas parents should consider and reflect upon themselves when helping build this quality in their children include:

- **Competence: The ability to handle situations effectively.** Ask yourself: Do I notice and praise what my child does well, or do I tend to focus on their mistakes? Do I communicate in a way that empowers them to make their own decisions, or do I end up lecturing them?

- **Confidence: The firm belief in one's abilities.** Ask yourself: Do I praise my child based on their efforts and achievements, or do I mainly focus on the outcomes of their performances? Do I support and treat them as a child learning to navigate their way through life, or do I undermine their growing independence?

- **Connection: Establishing a sense of belonging.** Ask yourself: How much quality, screen-free time does our family spend together? Do I allow my child to express all their emotions openly in front of me, and do I make an effort to understand and support them?

- **Character: A fundamental sense of right and wrong.** Ask yourself: Do I let my child develop their own set of values, or do I impose mine upon them? Do I consistently model positive character traits for them to learn from?

- **Contribution: Thinking and acting in ways that improve the world.** Ask yourself: Do I demonstrate generosity in my actions? Do I teach my child the importance and value of helping others?

- **Coping: Knowing how to deal with stress and put things in perspective.** Ask yourself: Do I help my child understand the difference between a true emergency and something that just feels urgent? Do I show them how to solve problems step-by-step when faced with challenges?

- **Control: Allowing your child to make decisions and understand that they can control the result.** Ask yourself: Do I reward my child when they take on more responsibility? Do I help them recognize and celebrate their small successes?

By thoughtfully addressing these key areas, parents can equip their children with the skills and mentality needed to not only navigate their way through competitive sports, but many of life's challenges with confidence and strength.

CHAPTER ONE: THREE KEY POINTS I NEED TO WORK ON

I Need To:

1. _____
2. _____
3. _____

How I'll Do It:

1. _____
2. _____
3. _____

When I'll Check My Progress:

1. _____
2. _____
3. _____

TWO
DEVELOPING YOUR MENTAL GAME PLAN

Imagine you're playing a game of basketball. You steal the ball mid-court and make a pass to a teammate on your right. Instantly, you cut left, sprinting towards the baseline. Your teammate spots your open path and throws the ball back to you. With two quick dribbles, you set yourself up for a spectacular windmill dunk, brimming with confidence. Ready to wow the crowd, you look up, but to your amazement—there's nothing there…

The hoop is missing and you do not have a target!

In that split second of confusion, you realize the importance of having a clear goal. Without it, all your efforts have no purpose, direction, or objective.

In basketball, every shot and pass you make is guided by the presence of a hoop. It's your focus point—your goal.

It's the same thing as being a student-athlete. Setting goals serves as your guiding light. Without them, you're left drifting aimlessly, unsure of where to direct your efforts, talents, and ambitions.

Let's break down why having goals are essential:

Focus: Setting goals helps you focus on what's most important during a game or practice. It gives you a target to aim for, and allows you to focus all your energy on reaching that target rather than being distracted by things that aren't going to benefit you.

Motivation: Goals give you something to work toward. They help feed your motivation and enthusiasm to work hard every day. Each goal you achieve builds upon the intrinsic drive you need to challenge yourself further and reach new heights.

Performance: Goal setting is the key to improving your performance. Let's say you're a swimmer and want to beat your personal best time in the 100-meter freestyle. By setting and working toward specific goals, you'll push yourself harder during training sessions. This will lead to better results—and a great sense of achievement when you set that new PR!

HOW TO SET SMART GOALS

In Chapter One, we explored having a growth mindset and were introduced to the concept of SMART goals. Do you remember what the SMART acronym stands for?

Let's recap:

- **S** is for specific.
- **M** is for measurable.
- **A** is for achievable.
- **R** is for relevant.
- **T** is for time-bound.

Let's learn more about each of these aspects for successful goal setting.

Specific

Your goal has to be specific to be worthwhile. Our minds work best when they are focused. A clear and specific goal drives action because we know exactly where we are headed. Here's a quick exercise to demonstrate the importance of having a specific rather than a general goal:

- Set your phone's timer for 15 seconds, and then list as many foods as you can.
- Now, reset it for another 15 seconds and write down as many healthy foods as possible.

I'll bet your second list was longer. That's because your mind was more focused.

Most people aren't great at setting goals. What they think are goals are just vague ambitions, like losing weight or doing better at math. Only when these vague ideas are broken down do they have any meaning.

Here are three examples of specific goals that a young athlete might set:

1. Improve my free throw accuracy.
2. Improve my soccer passing skills with my weaker foot.
3. Improve my tennis serve technique.

Measurable

Remember when I asked you to imagine playing basketball without a hoop? It didn't stop you from playing on the court, but it did prevent you from measuring your success. And, if you can't do that, there's not much point in playing the game.

It's the same with goal setting. You'll only know if you've achieved your goal if you can measure it. Let's return to the three goals we just set:

1. Improve my free throw accuracy.
2. Improve my soccer passing skills with my weaker foot.
3. Improve my tennis serve technique.

Something needs to be added to these goals—can you see what it is?

None of them can be measured. How will you know when you've achieved your free-throw accuracy goal? Your goal is only meaningful if you set targets that help you measure your progress. So, let's make these goals better by adding a measurable element:

1. Improve my free throw accuracy by 20%.
2. Make 15 successful passes with my weaker foot during a game.
3. Increase the speed of my tennis serve to reach a velocity of 90 mph consistently.

Wow, what a difference! Now you've got something to aim for. That's because what gets measured gets done!

Achievable

What do you notice about the measurable element we've just added to our goals?

They're realistic, right?

Imagine if, instead of improving your free throw accuracy by 20%, you set the goal of making it 80%. Does that sound achievable? Or does it seem unrealistic?

Unrealistic goals can be worse than not having a goal at all. They can turn you off, making you feel like there's no way I can achieve that, so I'm not even going to try.

Now, I'm not saying you will never improve your free throws by 80%. What I am saying is that you should set smaller, more achievable goals along the way. Each of these mini-goals will get you a step closer to your ultimate goal.

Each goal you set should challenge and push you just outside of your comfort zone, but it should not be so hard that it makes you feel overwhelmed or discouraged.

Relevant

Your goal should always be relevant to your sport.

Let's say you're a sprinter.

Your coach gives you a weight-training program to strengthen your quads, hamstrings, glutes, and calves. But when you turn up in the weight room, your friends are crowded around the bench press. You soon get caught up in the competitive atmosphere and peer pressure. Before you know it, you're all about bench pressing 200 pounds.

Sure, you turn up to do your leg workout, but that's not what really motivates you. While bench pressing might seem impressive in the weight room and still be of benefit as a sprinter, it's not the most relevant strengthening exercise for your sport.

Unless your goals are relevant, they don't belong in your training program.

Time-Bound

Let's check back to the three sample goals we've set:

1. Improve my free throw accuracy by 20%.
2. Make 15 successful passes with my weaker foot during a game.
3. Increase the speed of my tennis serve to reach a velocity of 90 mph consistently.

They're good, but something still needs to be added. Can you see what it is?

There's no time frame.

Okay, so you want to improve your free throws by 20%. Great, but when do you want to do that?—in the next week, three months, or five years?

You must set a clear deadline for your goal and stick to it. So, let's make the final tweak to our goals to make them perfect:

1. Improve my free throw accuracy by 20% within the next 6 weeks.
2. Make 15 successful passes with my weaker foot during a game within the next four matches.
3. Increase the speed of my tennis serve to reach a velocity of 90 mph consistently over the next 6 months.

It's essential to set a realistic time frame. Remember, you want that goal to be challenging but achievable. So, your gut feeling should be, "Yeah, I can do that, but it's going to take commitment and hard work."

SHORT & LONG TERM GOALS

Now that we've broken down the SMART goal formula, let's examine how to use it effectively throughout the year. Short-term goals build upon each other to bring you closer to your longer-term goals.

When you break down a longer-term goal to a daily level, you have something specific to focus on that day. So long as you can achieve your daily goal, the long-term goal will take care of itself.

Short-Term Goals

Daily: These are small goals you can achieve in a single day. It could be practicing a specific move for a set amount of time or eating a healthy snack after practice.

Example: Practice passing a ball with my weaker foot for 20 minutes after school.

Weekly: These goals are a bit bigger and last for a week. Maybe it's about increasing your repeat sprint ability or attending all your scheduled workouts.

Example: Increase my repeat sprint ability by adding one extra 20 meter sprint in at the end of each set during training this week.

Monthly: These goals last for a whole month. You might set goals like improving your ball control skills or running a certain distance without stopping.

Example: Increase the number of times I can juggle a soccer ball to 50 repetitions without it dropping by the end of the month.

Long-Term Goals

Quarterly: These goals last for three months at a time. It's a chance to see how much you've improved over a longer period. For example, you could aim to score a certain number of goals in your soccer games or run a faster time in your races.

Example: Decrease my average race time by 1.0-1.5 seconds in the 800m middle distance event over the next three months.

Preseason: These are the goals you set before your sports season starts. It's all about getting ready and practicing hard before your competitive season begins. Preseason is a perfect time to focus on improving those aspects of your game that you struggle with the most. This could include increasing your cardiovascular fitness, developing your tactical awareness, improving upon a specific technical skill, or a combination of all three!

Example: Improving my 1v1 defensive skills through better body positioning, game awareness, and decision-making.

Season: You want to achieve these goals during your sports in-season. It could be winning a championship, scoring a certain number of points, achieving a personal best time, or helping your team make it to the playoffs.

Example: Achieving a personal best for the 100 m sprint.

Yearly: These are your big dreams for the whole year. It might include making it onto a representative team, improving your skills enough to move up to a higher level of competition, or setting a school record in your specialist event.

Example: Breaking the school record for long jump.

PROCESS VS. PERFORMANCE VS. OUTCOME GOALS

Goals can be divided into three types: these include process, performance, and outcome goals.

Process goals focus on actions, techniques or behaviors that are needed to achieve a desired outcome. For example, a goalkeeper might set a process goal of improving their reaction time through hand eye coordination drills. This type of goal allows for the athlete to be in control of the result without external factors influencing the outcome.

Performance goals compares your performance to results you have previously achieved, or would like to achieve. They are used to create standards or benchmarks that an individual can set themselves to measure their progress. For example, a goalkeeper might set a target of making six saves per game or to have a save success rate of 80% across an entire season.

Outcome goals are most often related to winning an event, championship, or achieving a specific rank or position. For a goalkeeper, this might include winning a tournament or being crowned goalkeeper of the year.

You should include all three types of goals in your goal-setting strategy. Each one plays a crucial role in guiding your progress and success. Process goals help you refine your skills and technique; performance goals provide tangible benchmarks for improvement; and outcome goals keep you focused on your ultimate objective.

By including all three types, you create a well-rounded approach that maximizes your chances of reaching your full potential as an athlete.

MONITORING PROGRESS

Setting goals is like making a plan for where you want to go. But sometimes, plans need to be adjusted. It could be that you get better at a skill faster than you thought, or you may face some challenges you didn't expect. Perhaps you need to work a little harder on a skill, or you and your coach realize that you should focus on something else entirely different—and that's okay!

Goals are not set in stone. They're more like guideposts to keep you on track. By continuously evaluating where you're at, you will ensure that your goals remain relevant and attainable, allowing you to adapt to new circumstances and continue progressing towards your ultimate objectives.

So, whether you check in with yourself weekly, or chat with your coach and teammates, remember to monitor your progress.

OVERCOMING MENTAL BLOCKS AND BARRIERS

Do you have times when it feels like something's holding you back from giving your best during competition? It could be that you've nailed a particular skill through months of practice, but when it comes to the game, you mess it up.

Maybe your mind was clouded with doubts, distractions, or fears. We call these mental blocks. Here are some common blocks or barriers to watch out for:

- **Fear of Failure:** Do you ever feel paralyzed by the fear of making mistakes or falling short of expectations?
- **Perfectionism:** Are you constantly striving for the perfect game, setting impossibly high standards for yourself?

- **Fear of Injury:** Does the thought of getting hurt hold you back from taking risks or pushing your limits?
- **Low Self-Confidence:** Do you struggle with believing in yourself and your abilities?
- **Analysis Paralysis:** Are you overwhelmed by overthinking every move and unable to make decisions quickly?
- **Difficulty Maintaining Focus:** Do distractions from the crowd or other players often distract your attention from the game?
- **Mental Fatigue and Burnout:** Are you feeling mentally drained and exhausted from the pressures of competition?

If any of these sound familiar, don't worry. Recognizing these barriers is the first step toward overcoming them.

Strategies for Breaking Through

Every successful athlete has had to overcome mental blocks to let their full potential shine. Here are some strategies to help you break through the mental barriers that may be holding you back:

Use Cue Words: Choose simple, positive cue words like "strong" or "present" to keep you focused and motivated during competitions. Repeat these words in your head throughout the game to keep yourself zoned in.

Many top athletes have used cue words in this same way. Here are some examples:

- Michael Jordan: Focus
- Serena Williams: Bounce
- Usain Bolt: Drive
- Tom Brady: Grind
- Simone Biles: Power
- Kobe Bryant: Next

Kobe's cue word helped him move on from mistakes and focus on the next play.

Focus on What You Can Control: Try to avoid focusing on the things you can't control, like the weather, the crowd, or a poor referee's decision. Instead, shift your focus to what you can control—your mindset, preparation, and effort.

You must also focus on what you want to achieve, not what might go wrong. You've put all the hard work into practice; and now you have to execute. So, see yourself hitting that perfect shot. It's all about shifting your mindset from fear to confidence.

Now, when we talk about shifting your mindset, it really comes down to discipline. You can't always control what comes into your mind. For example, when you get the ball and are in a shooting position, sometimes you can't help the thought that "I'm going to mess this up." But you can make the decision not to dwell on it and replace it with a positive mindset.

So, whenever a negative thought pops into your head, kick it out. It doesn't belong there. Immediately replace it with a positive cue like "I've got this."

Block Distractions: Practice blocking out distractions by training your mind to focus purely on one task. This is a skill you can develop just like any other technical element of your sport. Here's an exercise to help you do it:

Sit in front of your TV, mute the volume, and hold your thumb up in front of the screen. Focus only on your thumbnail, ignoring the distraction of what's happening on the TV screen behind it. Do this for 15 seconds. Repeat daily until you can give a full minute's attention to your thumbnail without being distracted.

Another way to train yourself to block distractions is to play loud music or noises during your practice sessions. For example, put on a recording of a crowd clapping (or even booing!) while you're practicing your basketball free throws or free kicks in football.

Play for You: You're playing this sport because it's what you love. It's not to impress your classmates, please your parents, or keep your coach off your back. So stop trying to please all those other people. Don't let the fear of embarrassing yourself or letting others down hold you back.

Stay Present: Take a lesson from Kobe Bryant; he taught himself to focus only on what was happening in the present moment. What happened in the past minute was gone. What was about to happen in the next minute was irrelevant. All that mattered was what he was going to do in the next 15 seconds.

THE ROLE OF MENTAL PREPARATION

All the physical training and long hours spent perfecting your skills aren't going to mean anything if you can't handle the pressure of competition. That's why you need to put time into mentally preparing yourself to meet that challenge. By employing strategies like visualizing success and practicing mindfulness, you can ensure that your mind is just as ready as your body is to perform when it matters most.

So, let's talk about brain training. We can divide the brain into two parts:

- The conscious
- The subconscious

The conscious brain is where thinking happens. You're using it right now as you process these words. It's also where memories are stored.

The subconscious brain is the part that allows you to do things without thinking. It controls muscle memory, allowing you to operate on autopilot. If you've ever heard of top athletes operating "in the zone," their subconscious brain has taken over and they're able to perform without conscious thought.

A classic example was Michael Jordan in Game 5 of the 1997 NBA Finals. Jordan went into the game with what everybody thought at the time was the flu (years later however, it was revealed that he was suffering from food poisoning). Still, nobody would have known it—he scored 38 points which also included the last second game winning shot!

Here's what Jordan said after the win:

> *"The game was on autopilot. It was just happening. I was just out there, doing what I do."*

Jordan had trained for thousands of hours, and a part of his brain called the cerebellum remembered it so well that he didn't even have to think about what he was doing.

Your goal when competing is to allow your subconscious brain to take over so that you're acting without consciously thinking about it. When you can do that, you won't have to worry about overthinking or messing up because you'll be on autopilot—just like Mike!

So, how do you activate the subconscious brain while deactivating the conscious parts when you're competing?

That's simple: You practice—a whole lot!

The more you practice a skill, the more you will "burn it into" your cerebellum so that your autopilot kicks in when it counts.

At the same time, you've got to control your conscious brain. Trust in your training and tell your conscious brain to get out of the way so the subconscious part can do its thing.

It really comes down to getting out of your own way. Here are a couple of tips to help you do it:

Know Your Triggers: We all have triggers that set us off. You've got to identify what yours are. It could be something at home before you get to the game, or maybe it's a certain opposition player or something your coach says.

The best way to identify your triggers is to keep a self-reflection journal. Write down how you feel before, during, and after a game or practice session. Include what made you feel that way, then at the end of the week, review your journal and look for patterns of what your triggers might be.

Once you've identified what these are, make a plan to get rid of it. This may involve talking it over with your parents or coach, or implementing strategies like breathing techniques to calm your conscious mind.

Focus on the Process, Not Outcome: You play the game to win, but you mustn't let that outcome overburden you. The pressure to win can build up so that it stops you from playing your natural game. Instead, focus on what you need to do in the present moment and let the outcome take care of itself.

VISUALIZATION

Visualization is a mental training tool many of the world's best athletes use to improve their performance. It involves creating a realistic mental image of yourself performing in whatever the upcoming competition may be. Visualisation allows you to create a movie in your mind, complete with all the sights, sounds, and emotions of the real thing.

It provides you with the ability to run through a mental script of how you want things to unfold in the heat of competition. When you're in the middle of the action, you don't want to think about what you need to do. You'll recall that the conscious brain needs to be turned down so that the subconscious brain allows your instincts to take over. Visualization works alongside lots of technique and skills practices to allow this to happen.

Some people however find the very idea of visualization a bit weird—even cringy! They might consider it nothing more than wishful thinking. If that's how you feel, I need you to have an open mind on this one.

Visualization is not some airy, fairy-like mystical idea. Study after study has proven it works. It's also used by nearly every successful professional athlete on the planet. So, if it's good enough for the superstars of your sport, it's probably something you should take seriously, right?

Visualization will help you handle pressure. Effective visualization however doesn't just include things going to plan flawlessly. That's a vital part of it, but to really get you prepared, you should also visualize situations when things don't go your way. See yourself reacting instinctively, adjusting, and getting directly into the next play.

That's what swimming legend Michael Phelps did. He once told a reporter, "When I would visualize, it would be what you want it to be, what you don't want it to be, what it could be. You are always ready no matter what comes your way."

The really cool fact about visualization is that our brains react to real, as well as repeated mental imaginary in much the same way. For example, if you visualize yourself successfully kicking a penalty a hundred times, you are going to feel very confident when you actually step up to take that kick in real life.

…So, are you ready to give visual imagery a try?

Here's a handy acronym to help us remember how to do it:

PETTLEP

It stands for the following:

- **P**hysical
- **E**nvironment
- **T**ask

- Timing
- Learning
- Emotion
- Perspective

To walk us through, let's use the example of a young golfer to see how to apply each of the PETTLEP steps:

Physical: Make a vivid picture of every aspect of yourself about to hit the ball. Imagine that you're wearing your golf clothing. See yourself selecting your club, walking up to the ball, what it feels like gripping the club in your hands, looking at where you want to drive the ball up the fairway, building your stance, and then looking down at the ball.

Environment: Imagine the crowd, the trees, the wind, and the fairway stretching out ahead of you. Hear the hush of the crowd falling silent, smell the fresh air, and feel the ground underneath your feet.

Task: Focus on the actions required to hit the ball. Think about your backswing and downswing, connecting with the ball, then finally wrapping it up with the perfect follow-through to watch the ball gliding effortlessly down the middle of the fairway.

Timing: The time it takes to make the shot in your mental movie should be the same as in real life. As you move from one hole to the next, your shots should take the same amount of time.

Learning: Your mental imagery should evolve to include new skills you have developed. For example, as your putting improves, you must create a new mental script to include this enhanced ability.

Emotion: Imagine the emotions that you'd feel in a real-life situation. Include the feeling of both winning and losing, hitting a great shot, and missing an easy putt. This will help you fully prepare for what you may encounter on the golf course.

Perspective: As you look down, see your hands, the club, and the ball from your own internal point of view. Then, watch yourself as if you are a spectator standing a few feet away. By visualizing the task from both an internal and third-person point of view, it can help enhance self-awareness as well as what your overall technique looks like.

Let's now look at how to use visualization to help you get ready for challenges you've faced previously when competing. There are three steps to this process:

Step One: Write down three areas where you have struggled in the past. It could be that you overthink a play and then mess it up, or you get frustrated when a play doesn't come off and you lose focus for the next 30 seconds. Whatever the issues are, grab a pen and note them down here:

Issue No.1:

Issue No.2:

Issue No.3:

Step Two: Find a place without distractions and sit or lie down. Close your eyes and allow your body to relax completely. Now, create a vivid image of yourself in a competitive situation where you normally have the first issue on your list. Use PETTLEP to make the image as accurate as possible. The emotions should be so real that your heart rate increases, and your hands get sweaty.

Step Three: As you face the challenging situation, flip the script so that you respond in the way you want rather than how you're used to. For example:

- Instead of freezing up when you overthink a play, visualize yourself quickly adapting and confidently making split-second decisions, trusting your instincts to guide you through the situation flawlessly.
- Rather than getting frustrated and upset when a play doesn't go as planned, envision yourself maintaining a calm demeanor and immediately refocusing on the task at hand, channeling that frustration into a renewed determination to succeed.

Once you've successfully visualized how to handle your first issue move onto the next following the same process. The more you practice coping with multiple challenges the less likely you will find these situations will bother you during competition, leading to a more confident and seamless performance.

Visualization Practice

Visualization is a powerful training tool, but like any other technique, it is only effective when used consistently. I encourage you to start making it a regular practice, ideally on a daily basis.

The best time to practice visualization is when you can dedicate focused attention to it without distractions. Many athletes visualize early in the morning while lying in bed. In addition to all the other benefits of visualization, it also helps establish a positive tone for the rest of your day.

Others, like Michael Phelps, engage in visualization before going to sleep at night. Often they include a review of their day, reinforcement of their goals, and mental preparation for the next day's activities.

Practicing visualization techniques before training and competition can also be invaluable, and is often a vital part of every pro athlete's mental warm-up routine. We will however delve into more detail about visualization techniques for training and competition in later chapters.

PARENT'S CORNER: VISUALIZATION

Visualization is a powerful skill your child should consider adding to their mental training toolkit. For that to happen, you need to be on board with this practice. You may, however, be wondering if there is any sound basis to support its inclusion.

Well, here are a few studies to put your mind at ease:

A 2022 study published in the American Journal of Multidisciplinary Research and Innovation analyzed several peer-reviewed visualization papers. The researchers concluded that visualization is "a fantastic tool that they (athletes) may utilize to establish the mentality needed to attain long-term and short-term goals and (coaches should) teach younger athletes visualization … in a way that's easily accessible and fun for them."

A further study explored the relationship between mental imagery, physical maturity, and sporting performance among 40 male soccer players aged 10-17. The research assessed their ability to change direction after using mental imagery and found that more physically mature players demonstrated superior directional changes. In contrast, younger athletes who had yet to reach physical maturity showed less efficacy in their performance. This led the authors to recommend early implementation of mental imagery training to help improve performance in younger athletes whose neuromuscular pathways are still developing.

Finally, a 2019 systematic review of research examined 20 previous studies involving 835 participants who represented 12 different sports. All of these studies assessed the impact visualisation training had on performance. Skill improvement was shown across all sports, with longer-duration visualization programs producing greater improvements. There was also no difference in skill enhancement between novice, intermediate, and elite athletes. The researchers concluding that, "Imagery has proven to be an incredibly versatile technique for the development of sport-related skills. The present review supports using imagery for skill development, with results showing its effectiveness across a range of skills and abilities."

THE POWER OF ROUTINE

All teams and athletes go through a warm-up routine before competing. It usually involves a bit of light jogging, some dynamic stretching, and a series of agility drills. But have you ever considered your mental warm-up?

…Not that many players do.

Yet, if you want to overcome the mental challenges of competition, you've got to have a pregame routine that helps you prepare mentally for it.

The more consistent your mental preparation is, the more consistent your performance is going to be. Your pregame routine should include the following strategies:

1. **Switching on your focus:** Remind yourself of your game objectives and what you will focus on when you play. As we've already discussed, you should focus on the moment, not the outcome.
2. **Fuel your confidence:** Think about all the reasons why you're set to perform well—all the practice, skill development, and determination you've shown. Trust in your

coach and your teammates, knowing they've got your back and you've got theirs.
3. **Visualize your performance:** Sit comfortably, close your eyes, and mentally rehearse your performance. See yourself performing skillfully, executing tasks with ease, and succeeding.
4. **Trust in your skills:** Remind yourself that you've done the groundwork; trust in your training, and that now is the time to get out there and execute.
5. **Embrace the butterflies:** Everyone experiences what we call "butterflies" in the moments before a game. Your heart rate beats faster, and your palms get a little sweaty. It means that your body is getting ready to perform. Instead of thinking of these pregame butterflies as negative, embrace that they are there to give you the adrenaline boost needed to perform at your best.

Creating a pre-competition routine that's just right for you is super important. It's like having your own special recipe for success.

To help make this happen, try different things during your pregame warm-up. See what helps you feel the most ready and confident. It could be doing mental exercises, stretching a certain way, or listening to your favorite music.

As you gain experience and learn more about yourself, you'll figure out what techniques prepare you best for competition.

So keep experimenting, stay open to trying new things, and remember to tweak your routine as you go.

CHAPTER TWO: THREE KEY POINTS I NEED TO WORK ON

I Need To:

1. _____
2. _____
3. _____

How I'll Do It:

1. _____
2. _____
3. _____

When I'll Check My Progress:

1. _____
2. _____
3. _____

THREE
TECHNIQUES FOR EVERYDAY TRAINING

So far, we've explored powerful strategies to help you stay focused and let your skills shine during competition. In this chapter, we take a step back to explore techniques to boost your everyday training.

So much of your time in sport is spent training. It's where you develop the skills you need to succeed in competition. Unless you can develop a strong training mentality, you'll likely find maintaining consistency with your workouts challenging, potentially leading to missed sessions. You may also be thrown off when you struggle to nail a new skill or when your coach points out an area for improvement.

Therefore it's crucial to establish a strong training mindset to keep you on track day to day.

THE POWER OF POSITIVE SELF-TALK

Believe. —Ted Lasso

We talk to ourselves all the time. You're probably doing it right now. Sometimes, the things we tell ourselves are not very encouraging. This negative self-talk is like a literary critic inside our mind—one who doesn't like us very much!

This inner talk can really affect your performance, whether in practice or during competition. Imagine stepping up to take a penalty kick in soccer. If your inner talk is filled with doubts and criticisms like—"I always miss these" or "I'm not good enough"—chances are, your performance will suffer. On the other hand, if you approach the situation with positive self-talk—"I've practiced this countless times" or "I can do this!"—you're more likely to rise to the occasion.

You can probably recognize that negative self-talk is part of a fixed mindset. Yet, as we've already discovered, you can ditch that mentality and replace it with a growth mindset. Part of the process involves removing those negative thoughts in your head and replacing them with positive self-talk.

Positive Reframing

To be a successful athlete you must control your self-talk. However, that doesn't mean you can completely stop negative thoughts from entering your mind. But you can challenge these thoughts and flip it. It's called positive reframing.

Let's say you're practicing your three-point shot during basketball practice. You keep missing. It starts to get you frustrated, and the thought that "I suck at this. There's no point trying!" comes to mind. However, instead of fixating on it, change it.

Think of times when you've struggled with a skill, practiced hard, and improved. Remember how satisfying it felt to see progress and achieve your goals? Remind yourself that every missed shot is an opportunity to learn and grow. Instead of dwelling on the negative, reframe the situation positively.

Tell yourself, "I may be struggling now, but with practice and determination, I can master this shot." By shifting your perspective, you empower yourself to overcome challenges and continue striving for success.

Sanya Richards Ross is a four-time Olympic gold medalist in the 400-meter dash and the 4x400-meter relay. She began learning about positive reframing after placing third in the 400 meters at the 2008 Olympics despite being the overwhelming favorite to win gold. Here's Sanya talking about how positive reframing helped her at the 2012 Olympics where she claimed gold:

When I had a negative thought about "Well, you didn't do it in 2008," I would say, "Yeah, that's right, but I'm doing it today!" He [her sports psychologist] taught me how to fight negativity... with positivity, and so then you change your thought processes around to saying: I've had a great season, I've beat all these girls before, I'm prepared, I'm deserving!

Positive Reframing Exercise

Positive self-talk isn't natural. When we do something wrong, our natural reaction is to say something like, "Wow, I can't believe I stuffed that up—I'm so hopeless!"

The only way to change that natural reaction is to train for it. Just like you repeat a physical skill thousands of times until it becomes automatic, so, too, you've got to practice, repeat, and memorize positive self-talk.

The first step is to list three negative thoughts you say to yourself. This may include outrightly negative things like "I suck at this!" or it could be less obvious, like "I wonder what the coach is thinking" or "I hate playing in front of this referee."

These thoughts will lower your confidence and stop you from performing at your best. So, write them down:

1. _____
2. _____
3. _____

Now, create an alternative list that reframes each negative as a positive. Here are a few examples based on my negative statements a minute ago:

- "I suck at this" becomes "I can do this."
- "I wonder what my coach is thinking" becomes "I'm focused on me."
- "I hate playing in front of this referee" becomes "I'm in control of my performance."

Write down your alternative list here:

1. _____
2. _____
3. _____

Your job now is to repeat your positive statements to yourself every single day—not just once, but as many times as you can. You want to memorize those sentences so that they become second nature to you.

What you're doing here is altering your natural thought patterns. You are making the positive statements much more natural to say and think. They'll come to you automatically, even under the pressure of a game situation or when you're in the middle of a practice that's not going well.

This positive reframing is a powerful tool, but it only works if you practice it regularly. That means you've got to keep up memorizing those positive statements, not just for a few days but for weeks until they become your go-to thought patterns. You must actively repeat them to yourself during practices and games.

FOUR TYPES OF SELF-TALK

There are four types of self-talk to know about in sports. These include:

1. Calming ("Breathe in")
2. Instructional ("Control the ball")
3. Motivational ("You've got this")
4. Focus ('Next play")

You need to know which type to use in different situations. So, let's give it a try. For each of the four situations below, I want you to write the self-talk number from above you feel best matches it:

[ ] Situation A: You've just received the basketball and are about to drive forward for a layup

[ ] Situation B: It's 20 seconds to game time, and the band has just played the national anthem.

[ ] Situation C: You step up to take a penalty shot in soccer.

[ ] Situation D: You lose the ball to an opposition player.

There are no right or wrong answers here. You'll likely use more than one type in each situation. For example, when driving to the basket, you might start with a motivational message, like "you've got this," and then switch to instructional, like "control the ball."

By the way, there's some interesting research about how we address ourselves when using self-talk. Researchers at the University of Michigan asked test subjects to prepare for a speech but only gave them five minutes to do it. One group was told that when they talked to themselves as they prepared, they should use the first-person pronoun "I." The other group was told to use the second-person pronoun "you."

At the end of the five minutes, the researchers asked the subjects what they had said to themselves.

Well, guess what?

The people who had used "I" were more negative in their self-talk. They said things like:

- "I can't do this; it's not enough time."
- "I suck at speeches."
- "I need days to prepare for something like this."

But the people who used "you" were far more positive, with comments like:

- "You can do this."
- "You just need to focus."
- "You're good at speeches."

Why the difference? The researchers think it was because when you talk to yourself as another person, you become your own coach. You create distance from yourself, which makes you feel less emotional.

The takeaway from this study is to experiment with using "you" instead of "I" in your positive self-talk. If that little trick works for you, great!

JOURNALING

As an athlete, the ability to record your training and competition performances can be invaluable. Highly personal, a journal allows you to reflect not only upon your physical performance, but also gives you the opportunity to express your thoughts and feelings. These can include the excitement of winning a game, or the disappointment and frustration that comes with sustaining an injury.

Putting pen to paper can inspire, reset, and focus your mind. When thinking about what to write in your journal, ask yourself these types of questions:

- What aspects of today's practice/game went well for me?
- What specific actions or strategies contributed to my success?
- In what areas could I have performed better?
- What factors or challenges hindered my performance?
- What will I do to address these issues in the future?

Considering the above will help you maintain accountability for your day-to-day training, track performance patterns, and establish short and long term goals. Keeping a journal encourages consistent self-assessment and provides you with the opportunity to reflect on who you are (or want to be) as an athlete.

Gratitude Journaling

Gratitude involves displaying a positive attitude or appreciation for people, places, or other things in life that we recognize we are fortunate to have. A gratitude journal can help athletes develop a growth mindset, increase motivation, or put setbacks such as competitive losses or injury into perspective. The more you practice gratitude journaling, the more likely you are to feel less bothered by inconveniences and instead find a positive silver lining to focus your energy on.

For example, say your game gets delayed an hour because the opposition team is stuck in unexpected traffic. Instead of getting frustrated, use the time to bond more with your teammates, practice visualization techniques, or ask your coach questions about tactical plays your team has been working on.

When journaling, many athletes prefer to write their entries in the morning. It is a simple way of beginning the day with a positive outlook, which can, in turn, boost your mood for the day ahead. Alternatively, if done at night, it can allow you to reflect on what you were grateful for during that day or reframe any less-than-desirable performances or events that have occurred. This can mentally lighten your load and finish your day in an optimistic way before going to bed. Whatever time of the day suits you best is what you should go with; there is no right or wrong here.

If you are new to journaling, try to think of at least 3-5 people or things you are thankful for each day and provide as much detail as possible as to why. A good practice is to begin each gratitude entry with a statement like "I am thankful for" or 'I am grateful to have."

See below a few examples of what a gratitude journal entry might look like:

Gratitude Entry 1: I am thankful for my coach and his constant support. Especially today, when the opposition team scored a goal as a result of my mistake. Instead of being upset with me, his words of encouragement helped to keep me motivated and focused on what I needed to do for the rest of the game.

Gratitude Entry 2: I am grateful to have access to our indoor training facilities. Tonight it allowed my team to continue training instead of being cancelled due to the stormy weather.

Gratitude Entry 3: I am grateful to my parents for always preparing healthy meals for me after training or when I compete. It allows me to rehydrate and replenish my body with the nutrients I need to recover and keep me performing at my best.

Although these examples may seem trivial, practicing gratitude can help you better appreciate the things that you may sometimes take for granted. It can also help you to maintain a better perspective when faced with setbacks not only within sports, but life in general.

HARNESSING THE BENEFITS OF MINDFULNESS AND MEDITATION

You may have heard of mindfulness. Over the past few years it has become a popular strategy to promote mental awareness. Mindfulness involves paying attention to what's happening inside your mind and the world around you. It also requires that your attention be focused on the present moment.

That means not thinking about things that have already happened, like mistakes, or wondering what will happen in the future, like winning or losing. You are entirely focused on what is going on right now.

The goal of mindfulness isn't to think about nothing. It's to allow thoughts to pass you by like clouds, without making judgments about them. You can also think of it like watching cars go by on a busy highway. You don't get in the car; just watch it drive past.

Compare that to how most people react to thoughts. To continue the analogy, they flag the car down, get in, and drive off to somewhere they weren't planning to go. They have allowed themselves to get distracted and carried away by that one thought.

When this happens during training or competition, your mind and body go in different directions. Your body is moving forward, but your mind has wondered off somewhere else. That is not going to work out well!

Research shows that mindfulness is a powerful skill for athletes. A 2020 study examined the effect of mindfulness practices on endurance and skill performance. Forty-six university athletes were divided into two groups. One group was given a five-week mindfulness training program, while the other was not.

Results demonstrated that the mindfulness group had significantly higher levels of endurance during competition. They could also execute skills with greater precision and made fewer errors during practice and competitive events.

There are three fundamental principles of mindfulness. These involve:

1. Not judging
2. Accepting
3. Patience

Not judging isn't natural. We have to train ourselves to do it, and need some mental tools and tricks to make it happen. One of these tricks is to have a "cleansing tool." This is something you concentrate on to act as your refocus point.

Let's look at an example:

Say you're a rugby lock, and you've just broke free from a scrum. The thought comes to your mind that the opposing player intentionally headbutted you. You can either dwell on that thought and let your anger build, or use mindfulness to just let the thought pass you by.

So, you decide to use your cleansing tool to put the situation behind you. To do this you've selected a spot on the field, like the bottom of the goalpost. You focus, just for a second, on this spot, and it acts as a recentering tool. It reminds you to not dwell on the thought but to practice deep breathing and positive self-talk.

For this to work, you must choose what your cleansing tool will be before the competition starts. This doesn't necessarily have to be something like a spot on the filed either. It can be anything from a piece of jewellery you are wearing, to a physical act like tapping your heels together. So long as it is something you can use repetitively and allows you to reset, then go with whatever works best of you.

Acceptance is about not beating yourself up about for you've just done. Accept it and move on to the next task. Remember Kobe Bryant? What was his favorite cue word? Go back to Chapter Two and check if you can't remember.

Developing a nonjudgmental frame of mind and acceptance takes time. That's where **patience** comes in. You can't just practice it a few times and expect to nail it. Our minds are often geared toward negativity, so changing the script takes real effort!

Mindfulness vs. Meditation

Mindfulness is not the same as meditation. Mindfulness is a skill, while meditation is a tool for developing that skill. There are many types of meditation, with Western Vipassana meditation being a popular method for athletes.

This type of meditation focuses on your breath as it enters and leaves your body. When your mind wanders, you bring your attention back to your breathing each time. This repeated practice strengthens your ability to stay present and enhances overall mindfulness. It is an easy form of meditation to use anytime, anywhere, especially as an athlete.

The Three "A's" of Mindfulness

Developing the skills need for mindfulness can be broken down into three steps:

1. **Awareness**. Imagine you're standing on the side of the highway, watching cars go by. You notice the makes, models, and colors. Do the same with your thoughts, identifying the negative self-talk.
2. **Acceptance.** Accept the situation you're in and what is happening; don't argue about it in your head. Acknowledge

the thoughts and feelings you are experiencing rather than ignoring or denying them.
3. **Adjustment.** Now that you've accepted what's happening, adjust your attitude or focus as needed to change your mentality. This could include turning negative self talk into a positive affirmation using your cue words.

Having visual cues to remind you to apply these three steps throughout the day can be helpful. Visual cues might include sticky notes with the three "A" words written on them. Place these on your mirror, in your school textbooks, and in other places where you'll see them as you go about your daily activities.

Another visual cue is something you wear, like a wristband, colored shoestring, or a particular pair of socks. Every time you look at this item, it will remind you to put the three A's into action. This is particularly beneficial when you are training or competing.

MEDITATION TECHNIQUES

Here are three meditation techniques you can start using to help develop mindfulness. There's no set amount of time you should spend on this, but the more often you do it, the more natural your mindful thinking will become. Start with a few minutes each day and build from there.

Meditation may not come naturally to you, so it's important to be patient with yourself. If your mind begins to wander, gently guide your focus back to the present moment without judgment.

- **Body Scan Meditation:** Lie comfortably and focus on different parts of your body. Start with your toes and gradually move up toward your head. Notice any areas of discomfort or tension, consciously trying to relax those muscles as you continue scanning. This practice helps cultivate body awareness and relaxation.

- **Mindful Walking Meditation:** Take a leisurely walk inside or outdoors, and pay close attention to each step you take. Notice the sensations in your feet as they contact the ground, the movement of your legs, and the rhythm of your breath. If your mind starts to think of other things, gently redirect your focus back to the physical sensations of walking.
- **Breath Awareness Meditation:** Sit comfortably in a quiet place. Focus on your breath, paying attention to the sensations of each inhalation and exhalation and the rise and fall of your chest. Again, if your mind starts to wander, guide it back to the sensation of breathing without getting frustrated.

BREATHING EXERCISES TO CONTROL ANXIETY AND STRESS

We usually don't think about breathing. It's an automatic process that happens constantly. You know that if you stop breathing by holding your breath, you'll have problems after a while—like passing out!

But did you know that you can become a better athlete by actively controlling your breath? For decades, the world's top athletes have been using breathwork to control stress, anxiety, and get themselves in the zone.

Michael Jordan knew how important it was to use his breath to control his mind. He once commented, "Breathing techniques are important for athletes to master because they help calm the mind and reduce anxiety. In those tense moments on the court, deep breathing can help you stay focused and execute under pressure."

So, how does breathing help do all of these things?

When you feel stressed, like at the start of a game or when facing a tough opponent, your body goes into what's called "fight or flight mode." This is your body's natural response to threats. Your heartbeat will increase, your muscles will become tense, and your breathing will be faster and shallower.

Focused breathing allows you to control how your body reacts to stress. When you take slow, deep breaths, you signal to your brain that everything is okay. This activates your **parasympathetic nervous system**, which is the opposite of fight-or-flight.

The parasympathetic system helps your body relax and calm down. It slows down your heart rate, shifting your body from a state of heightened alertness to one of calm relaxation. At the same time, your muscles release tension and loosen up. You'll feel more physically relaxed, more flexible, and more agile.

The parasympathetic nervous system also influences your mind. By activating this system through controlled breathing, you can experience a sense of mental clarity and calmness. As your body relaxes, your mind becomes less preoccupied with worries and distractions. This allows you to focus more effectively on a task, whether it be playing on the field or solving a problem in the classroom.

FOUR BREATHING TECHNIQUES FOR YOUNG ATHLETES

Listed on the following pages are breathing techniques you can practice anywhere, anytime. I recommend using them during meditation to help you relax and become more mindful. You can also use these whenever you're stressed, whether in the classroom, at home, during practice, or while competing.

Start each training session with a few minutes of focused breathing to help you prepare. This may involve diaphragmatic or box breathing to center the mind and calm any pretraining jitters.

During training, use breathing techniques during breaks. For example, you might practice rhythmic breathing to help you catch your breath between sets and reps in the weight room.

At the end of training, unwind with a minute or two of visualization combined with diaphragmatic breathing to help aid with recovery and mental rejuvenation.

You can also add breathing exercises into your warm-up routine. Start with gentle cardio or dynamic stretching, then move into rhythmic or box breathing exercises.

Diaphragmatic Breathing

- Sit or lie in a comfortable position.
- Put one hand on your chest and the other hand on your belly.
- Slowly breathe in through your nose, noticing your stomach rising as you fill your lungs with air. Try to keep your chest relatively still.
- Exhale slowly through your mouth, noticing your belly fall as you release as much air as possible from your lungs.
- Repeat this process several times, focusing on making each breath deep and smooth.

Box Breathing

- Imagine a square or a box with four sides.
- Inhale slowly and deeply for a count of four as you trace one side of the square with your mind's eye.
- Then, hold your breath for a count of four while tracing the second side of the square.
- Next, slowly exhale for a count of four as you trace the third side of the square.
- Finally, hold your breath again for a count of four as you complete the square.
- Repeat this process for several rounds, maintaining a steady pace. If you can't quite get to four seconds that's okay.

Rhythmic Breathing

- Find a comfortable rhythm for your breathing, such as inhaling for three counts and then exhaling for three counts.
- Focus on maintaining this rhythm throughout your breathing practice.
- You can adjust the count to suit your comfort level, but aim for a balanced and consistent pattern.
- Pay attention to the natural flow of your breath and try to synchronize it with your chosen rhythm.

The 4-7-8 Technique

- Sit down or lie in a comfortable position with your back straight.
- Place the tip of your tongue just behind your upper front teeth, keeping it there throughout the entire exercise.
- Close your mouth and inhale quietly through your nose for a count of four.
- Now hold your breath for a count of seven.
- Next, completely exhale out through your mouth, making a whooshing sound for a count of eight.
- Repeat this cycle for a total of four breaths.
- As you practice, try to relax your facial muscles and let go of any tension in your body.

ESTABLISHING A CONSISTENT TRAINING MINDSET

When it comes to training your mind, consistency is key. It helps you build discipline and boosts your confidence because you know you're putting in the work day in and day out. Consistent practice also helps toughen up your mind, making you mentally strong when the going gets tough during competition.

Just like you have a schedule for school and practice, having one for your mindset training is also essential.

Set aside some time each day to work on exercises that strengthen your mental game, including the visualization, positive self-talk, meditation, journaling, and breathing exercises we have discussed in this chapter. Studying the mindset of successful athletes you admire can also be beneficial. Learn about their routines, rituals, and mental strategies, then build those elements that resonate with you into your own routine.

CHAPTER THREE: THREE KEY POINTS I NEED TO WORK ON

I Need To:

1. _____
2. _____
3. _____

How I'll Do It:

1. _____
2. _____
3. _____

When I'll Check My Progress:

1. _____
2. _____
3. _____

FOUR
APPLYING MENTAL TOUGHNESS ON GAME DAY

You know that game day feeling—your heart races, your palms are sweaty, you get those "butterflies" in your stomach—knowing you must perform can sometimes get the best of you. Yet, as we've already seen, you have the power to harness that energy and turn it into your secret game day weapon.

In this chapter you'll discover the mental strategies of the world's best athletes to overcome game day jitters, transform nerves into excitement, and rise above the pressure to perform. From pregame rituals that get you in the zone to techniques for staying focused under fire, we'll discover the secrets to unlocking your full potential when it matters most.

PREGAME PREPARATION: GETTING YOUR MIND IN THE ZONE

What you do in the time leading up to competition can make or break your performance. It's too important to leave it to chance. That's why you need a pregame routine to ensure consistency.

All successful athletes have a pregame routine. Its purpose is to allow you to squeeze the maximum value from the hours and minutes leading up to competition to ensure you perform at your best.

Finding the ideal pregame routine for you takes time. You need to try different things, experiment with various strategies, and tweak the routine to discover what works best for you. But it should include both physical and mental preparation.

You could start with light stretching. Then, listen to your favorite pump-up playlist to get in the zone. Visualizing yourself dominating the competition can also help dial in your focus and boost your confidence.

Some athletes swear by specific rituals or superstitions, like wearing lucky socks or eating the same pregame meal every time before competing. While these might seem silly to some, they can be powerful tools for building consistency and getting your mind in the right place.

The key is to find what works best for you. You may thrive on high-energy activities like jumping jacks or shadowboxing, or perhaps you prefer quiet meditation to calm your nerves. Whatever it is, make it your own and stick with it.

However, remember your pregame routine is not set in stone. It's okay to adjust and adapt it as you go along. The goal is to find what helps you feel focused, confident, and ready to conquer the competition. If you feel something is no longer working for you, it's okay to change it.

Michael Jordan discovered that the best approach for him was to distract himself from the upcoming game by joking around, pranking his teammates, and listening to music. Then, right before the game, he'd switch focus and start challenging himself to be the best player on the court. He'd also repeat his cue word (focus) repeatedly to himself as he stepped out onto the court.

Rafael Nadal's pregame routine begins with a freezing cold shower 45 minutes before a match. Then, in the tunnel, he's constantly moving as he waits with his opponent to be called out onto the court. He performs short sprints, bounces, shuffles from side to side, practices his forehand and backhand. He'll then finish with a few vertical jumps immediately before walking out.

Rafa's routine not only primes him mentally and physically, but also affects his opponents. The other player is often shown standing there nervously, watching Nadal repeat his routine. They risk being psyched out by his energy before the game even starts!

PRE-PERFORMANCE ROUTINES

A pre-performance routine is a sequence of thoughts and actions you perform before executing a self-paced skill during competition. It could be prior to serving on the tennis court, or as you step up to the free-throw line in basketball.

Your pre-performance routine helps you stay focused in the moment. It should make you feel comfortable performing a routine you've done many times before, and help to control distractions.

So, how do you develop a killer pre-performance routine? Let's break it down:

- Start by pinpointing the specific actions that require focus and precision during your sport. Is it your serve, your shot, or your swing?
- Now, develop a specific routine. If you're at the free throw line, you might set your feet, dribble twice, look at the rim, repeat your cue word, and then execute the shot.
- Once established, it's now up to you to practice, practice, practice! Set aside time to run through your routine repeatedly until it becomes second nature. The more you practice, the more automatic it will feel when you're under pressure during a game.

Remember, your pre-performance routine is a powerful tool in your arsenal, but it's only effective if you use it consistently and with intention. So, practice it often, refine it as needed, and trust in its ability to help you perform at your best.

Rituals

Do you have a particular pair of socks you wear to every game? Or a favorite song you must play before stepping onto the court? If you do, then you've got a ritual. It's your own little trick to get you feeling super confident and pumped for competition.

Sports rituals can be anything from wearing a particular jersey to saying a special prayer. The key is to find what works best for you. You may have a lucky charm in your pocket or a pregame handshake with your teammates. Perhaps it's touching a particular landmark, like tapping your club's logo as you walk out of the locker room. Whatever the ritual is, own it and believe in its power to help you shine.

Here are some pretty interesting rituals that pro athletes have performed to give themselves a competitive edge:

- Michael Jordan wore his University of North Carolina shorts under his NBA uniform throughout his career as he felt they gave him good luck.
- Another former NBA athlete, Jason Terry, took things a step further by sleeping in his opponent's shorts before every game.
- A former college football coach, Les Miles, had a taste for turf—literally. Before every game, he would pluck a chunk of grass from the field and chow down.
- Minnie Minoso, a former MLB athlete, had a unique way of washing away a bad game. If things didn't go his way on the field, he blamed it on his uniform and wore it in the shower post-game to cleanse himself of any bad mojo.

EFFECTIVE TEAM COMMUNICATION

It's game day. You have worked hard on set plays, know the game plan, and are ready to make it happen. However, time and time again your team struggles to execute… Sound familiar?

Often, this can be due to one critical component:

Poor communication.

I have seen the performances of even the most physically talented and tactically aware teams suffer as a result of this often overlooked but vital aspect of team sports.

Effective communication is a cornerstone of any successful team. Good communication skills are not just about talking; they're also about listening and building trust. When you, your teammates, and coach communicate well, roles and responsibilities are easier to understand, reducing the likelihood of misunderstandings or outbursts of frustration during competition. This creates a more harmonious team environment where everyone feels supported and safe to express themselves without fear of judgment. This can help teams overcome challenges, stay focused under pressure, and continuously improve performance.

It is for these reasons that mastering this must have skill is important for any team sport athlete. When on the field, here are some handy tips to help you effectively communicate with your teammates:

Project your Voice: When other distractions can interfere with your teammates' ability to hear you, such as crowd noises, stadium echo's, or other games being played around you, the ability to project your voice is crucial. This makes sure your message reaches your intended teammates, minimizing the risk of misunderstandings and tactical errors.

Speak Clearly and with Confidence: If you have made a decision, or see something unfolding in front of you that requires communication with your teammates, deliver your message clearly and with confidence. This will signal to your teammates that you are either focused and ready to take action, or that they need to react. When you are decisive, respectful, and clear with your instructions, your teammates will know that you mean business, instilling a sense of confidence and trust in your ability.

Look for Nonverbal Cues: Not all communication during competition is verbal. Depending on your team's formation, playing style, and tactics, you must be able to read your teammates' body language and understand what their movements signal during set patterns of play. These nonverbal cues can provide you with important information on when and how you must respond. For example, a teammate opening up their body shape and making eye contact with you could signal, "Hey, I'm ready to receive the ball." Similarly, you might wait for a teammate to lift their head before timing a run in behind the opposition's defensive lines. Alternatively, if a teammate vacates space, this could be to intentionally provide you with the room you need to drive into. Nonverbal cues such as hand signals are also an effective way to communicate with teammates while at the same time concealing what your next move is from the opposition!

Practice: As a young athlete it can sometimes be daunting communicating with your teammates in the heat of competition. The fear of saying the wrong thing, or messing up a set play with poor communication may leave you feeling like it's best not to say anything at all. This is why making effective communication a habit at training is so important. The more you can practice and get comfortable with it away from the pressure of competition, the easier you will find communicating is when it matters most.

STAYING CALM AND COLLECTED DURING HIGH-PRESSURE MOMENTS

Have you ever watched your favorite athlete choke in a high-pressure situation? It could be your soccer hero blowing a penalty, your favorite NBA player missing a non-contested dunk, or your golf idol failing to sink an easy putt. If not, keep watching them—it's going to happen!

Yes, intense competitive pressure can even affect our sporting heroes, leading them to choke. Choking is when you freeze up because you let the moment's pressure get to you. You mess it up when you should have nailed it.

The opposite of the choke is the clutch. It's when you can brush off pressure, step up to the moment, and complete tasks with a successful outcome.

The most common cause of choking is over arousal. In other words, you are receiving too much mental and physical stimulation. The heightened stress stimulates the sympathetic nervous system, significantly increasing blood flow. Our heart rate increases, the pupils dilate, our blood pressure rises, and sweating increases.

These bodily reactions can make it difficult to focus on the fine motor skills you need to perform. The only way to prevent the choking that results from over arousal is to lessen your stimulation level. You still want a certain level of arousal to allow you to perform, but not so much that it throws you off your game.

Here are a few strategies that can help you stay calm and prevent over arousal during high-pressure moments:

Focused Breathing

During high pressure situations in sports, over arousal can add to your anxiety, causing your breathing to be shallow and fast. Deep breathing allows you to take control, relaxing your muscles, and controlling your mind.

Of course, you don't have time to do an extended breathing exercise when you're in a clutch-play situation. But you do have time to take a few deep breaths in through your nose and out through your mouth. Try to let go of any tense or anxious thoughts as you breathe. Imagine that with every exhale, you're releasing all that nervous energy. This will activate your parasympathetic nervous system, helping to lower your arousal level.

Below are three examples of pro athletes who harness the benefits of focused breathing during competition:

- **Novak Djokovic (Tennis):** Novak Djokovic, one of the greatest tennis players of all time is known for his meticulous approach to physical and mental preparation. He incorporates breathing techniques into his routine to manage stress and stay focused during matches. Djokovic has spoken about using deep breathing exercises to remain calm under pressure and keep his composure between intense rallies.

Here is how Novak summed it up:

"That is how I try to get myself back into an optimum state of mind and body. Through breathwork, conscious breathing, whether it's just one or two or five or ten breaths, depending on how much time I have... Just conscious breathing. It's as simple as that."

- **LeBron James (Basketball):** A basketball icon and multiple-time NBA champion, LeBron James emphasizes the importance of breathing exercises in his training regimen. James utilizes deep breathing techniques to stay centered and composed during high-pressure situations on the court. He credits controlled breathing for helping him maintain focus, manage fatigue, and regulate his emotions during games.

- **Simone Biles (Gymnastics):** Olympic gold medalist Simone Biles, incorporates breathing exercises into her pre competition routine to improve her performance. Biles utilizes rhythmic breathing techniques to calm her nerves, increase oxygen flow to her muscles, and improve her performance on the apparatus. She has mentioned using deep breathing to stay grounded and confident while executing complex gymnastics routines.

Singular Focal Point

Have you ever had someone tell you to stop worrying about competition pressure or to turn your mind off so that you shut it out? By now, you can see that it's not very good advice. You can't just turn your mind off. It's always thinking about something.

So, rather than telling your mind to stop worrying, distract it with something else. A fantastic way to do this is to find a singular focal point. You simply pick an object you can see, and then focus your attention on it during a high pressure moment. Let's look at an example:

Say you're a rugby player responsible for taking field goals. The score is tied and this is the last play of the game. In the moments leading up to the kick, you have the world's weight on your shoulders. Everyone in the crowd is watching your every move, and all your teammates are relying on you. Everything's riding on this kick to win the game.

No wonder your mind wants to wander. However, you don't let it; instead, you pick a spot to focus on—like the center point of the goalpost. Keep directing your mind back to that spot. Your whole mental energy is focused on the center of that bar. Even as you place the ball and step out your approach, you're still thinking about your focal point.

No matter what sport you play, find a single focal point that you can concentrate on. This will keep your mind busy so you're not thinking about any other distractions that could derail your performance.

Engage Your Senses

Pressure does not exist in the present moment. It comes from thinking about past mistakes or worrying about future ones. You must get into the present moment whenever you feel pressure during competition.

You can do this by fully engaging your senses. By concentrating on what you see, hear, or feel, you can shift your focus away from stressors and reduce anxiety. For example, concentrate on the look and feel of a basketball in your hands as you step up to take a free throw. Concentrate on details like the seams where the panels of the ball are stitched together and how the raised pebbly surface feels in your hands. When you run your fingers over the surface, can you feel the individual pebbles and seams, offering a combination of both rough and smooth. By concentrating on such details it can help you stay focused in the present moment, allowing feelings of pressure to fade away.

Tell yourself, "It's Just ..."

Here's a cue phrase so powerful that it deserves its own heading!

Whatever the skill is you are about to execute is something you've practiced hundreds, maybe thousands of times before, right?

If you look at it that way, it's no big deal.

So, tell yourself, "It's just a layup," "It's just a free kick," or whatever the action is that you're about to perform. That reminder will help remove pressure from the situation, allowing the skill you've worked so hard at to shine through.

MANAGING MISTAKES AND MOVING FORWARD

Do you find it hard to let go of mistakes during competition? Does that two-second fumble keep replaying in your mind like a movie, destroying your ability to stay present? Or does it hold you back from showing what you can really do out of fear of messing it up again?

It's crucial to develop strategies that allow you to regain your focus and confidence quickly, ensuring that a single error doesn't throw off your entire performance.

The following are what I call "Bounce Back" techniques to help you recover from mistakes and move forward:

Bounce Back Beliefs

Your thoughts can be your worst enemy in those moments following a mistake. That's where positive self-talk comes in. Instead of letting negative thoughts take over, use positive affirmations to keep your mind focused and maintain your self-belief. This could include simple statements like "Go again," "Next one," or "Level up." The time to reflect on why you made the mistake is after the game. Whilst you're still in the heat of competition believe that you have it within you to recover and keep going.

Bounce Back Body Language

After making a mistake, it's natural to drop your head, slump your shoulders, place your hands on your head, or slow down. This type of body language projects a sense of defeat and lack of confidence. Not only does this hinder your performance, but it also signals to your opponents, teammates, and coaches that you feel beat.

Some very fascinating research on body language has been conducted with professional tennis players on the ATP tour. During tie break points, researchers found a connection between nonverbal body language and players' subsequent performance. Negative or submissive body language was associated with a more undesirable performance, while positive or dominant body language led to a more successful next play.

Therefore, once you've made a mistake, don't let your body language drag you down further. What's done is done, so stand tall! This means head up, chest open, eyes forward, and move with purpose. These simple adjustments to your posture can do wonders to help you regain focus, build confidence, and give nothing away to the opposition.

Bounce Back Buddies

A bounce back buddy is someone you can rely on to keep you focused and encourage you after you've made a mistake. This person could be a teammate, your coach, or a family member watching in the crowd. Between the two of you, come up with a way of communicating when you need that boost of confidence. It could be as simple as a specific look, nod of the head, thumbs up, or word to comfort and remind you that you're not alone, they believe in you, and you've got this!

THE POWER OF PERSPECTIVE

After you've finished your game or event, your mistakes are likely to still come back and dominate your thoughts.

This is when you need to think about reframing. Reframing means stopping the self-criticism and looking for opportunities to improve. Reflect on the error and identify what you can take away from the experience. Did you rush your shot? Were you out of position? Use mistakes as feedback to refine your skills and become a better athlete.

Remember to always keep sight of the bigger picture. Your performance in one game or season does not define your worth as an athlete. Success isn't only about wins and losses; it's also about your growth, effort, and perseverance.

Maintaining a broader perspective allows you to keep setbacks in context and prevents you from getting discouraged by individual errors. Celebrate your successes, no matter how small, and recognize the progress you've made along the way. By focusing on the journey rather than the destination, you'll develop a resilient mindset that carries you through triumphs and challenges.

THE ART OF COMEBACKS: TURNING THE GAME AROUND

Successful athletes never give up. They have a mindset to grind it out to the end. They never tank. Instead, they find a way to adjust and mount a comeback. So, how do they do it? And, more importantly, how can you do it too?

You may have heard the expression, "When life gives you lemons, make lemonade." This expression means that you should accept the situation you're faced with and make the best of it. Whether it's an injury, or the fact that you're down by 20 points at halftime, the first step in your comeback has got to be acceptance of where you are.

The next step is to commit to turning things around. You've got to be stronger than that voice that tells you, "You're too far down" or "What's the point?" Don't just wish things were different—commit to making them different!

To do this you've got to put in the effort to make things happen. We can summarize this in three steps as follows:

- Accept the situation.
- Embrace the situation.
- Address the situation.

Taking these steps isn't easy. Staying positive can become a real struggle when you've fallen behind. The same is true when you suffer an injury. To prevent yourself from wallowing in pity, you've got to have three qualities:

- A growth mindset
- Self belief
- A positive attitude

The work you've done in previous chapters is helping you develop those qualities. So let's now look at some specific strategies to turn around a losing situation and make an incredible comeback.

Goal Resetting

Instead of focusing on the overall deficit or setback, break the situation down into smaller, more manageable goals. Set specific objectives for each quarter, half, inning, or distance and concentrate on achieving them one step at a time. By shifting your focus to achievable short-term goals, you can regain control of the situation and build confidence as you progress.

For example, let's say you're a tennis player who has just lost the first two sets. Rather than letting your mind wander to negative thoughts, force it to focus on strategic stepping stone goals such as holding serve. Concentrate on your technique, aiming for accuracy, consistency, and ball placement.

Next, target breakpoints. Look for opportunities to apply pressure, return aggressively, and exploit your opponent's weaknesses.

Focus on winning games, not sets. Your aim should be to win the next game, then the one after that, and so on. By approaching the match one game at a time, you can gradually chip away at the deficit and build momentum.

Stay present in the moment and maintain a positive attitude, focusing on the opportunities ahead rather than the setbacks behind. Visualize yourself executing your shots effectively, staying composed under pressure, and fighting for every point with determination and resilience.

Also take note of your opponent's strengths and weaknesses and change your strategy accordingly. Consider making tactical adjustments, such as changing your shot selection, changing the pace and spin of your shots, or approaching the net more frequently. The idea is to throw off your opponent, disrupting their rhythm to gain an advantage.

Strategic Visualization

During breaks in the game, visualize yourself executing successful plays, making crucial shots, or scoring decisive points. Imagine the sights, sounds, and sensations of success in vivid detail, reinforcing positive mental images of your performance. This mental rehearsal will help improve confidence, reduce anxiety, and enhance your ability to execute under pressure.

Maintaining Resilience

You must remain convinced that you have the situation under control and are surging toward inevitable victory. Remind yourself of past comebacks or victories, drawing strength from your previous successes and determination.

In these situations, camaraderie and mutual support are essential in team sports. Lean on your teammates for encouragement and inspiration, rallying together in the face of adversity. Build a culture of belief and resilience within your team, reminding each other of your collective potential and shared goals. Whether it's a reassuring pat on the back or a motivating pep talk, draw strength from the belief and trust in your teammates.

Embrace a team motto or favorite quote that sums up your team's values. Whether it's "United as One" or "Strength in Numbers," find a mantra that resonates with your team's identity and creates a sense of purpose and determination. Use this motto as a source of inspiration during challenging moments, reaffirming your commitment to each other and the pursuit of excellence.

RAFAEL NADAL'S STUNNING COMEBACK – 2022 AUSTRALIAN OPEN GRAND FINAL

In the 2022 Australian Open Grand Final, superstar tennis player Rafael Nadal faced a formidable opponent in the very talented Daniil Medvedev. Despite his incredible skill and experience, Nadal struggled in the early stages, making uncharacteristic errors and falling behind in the match.

During the first few games, Nadal was extremely nervous. Medvedev dominated, and it was almost impossible for Rafa to see a path to victory. The Spaniard lost the first two sets 6-2, 7-6, and Medvedev looked set to close out the match early in the third set.

However, one of Nadal's unique qualities is that he loves the fight. When things look hopeless, he excels; it's when he feels most alive and comfortable. Nadal began to use more slicing shots to bring Medvedev to the net. He began to win crucial points, causing Medvedev to doubt whether he was in control. With each point, Nadal fought back with unwavering determination, showcasing his trademark grit.

In a stunning display of mental strength, Nadal mounted an incredible comeback, turning the tide of the match in his favor and ultimately emerged victorious, winning the last three sets 6-4, 6-4, 7-5 in a match that lasted 5 hours and 24 minutes. At the time, the win made Nadal the most decorated male Grand Slam winner of all time. He now had 21 titles to his name, breaking a three-way tie he held with Roger Federer and Novak Djokovic of 20 Grand Slams each.

His remarkable resilience in the face of adversity is a powerful reminder of the importance of perseverance and self-belief.

Three Lessons from Rafa

Here are some invaluable takeaways to learn from Nadal:

- **Embrace the Fight:** Nadal's love for the fight highlights the importance of embracing challenges and competing with passion and determination, even when things seem hopeless.

Lesson: Learn to view adversity as an opportunity to showcase your skills and rise to the occasion rather than giving in. Setbacks and challenges are inevitable in sports, but how you respond to adversity defines your character and potential for success.

- **Adaptability and Strategic Thinking:** Nadal's strategic adjustment to incorporate more slicing shots to disrupt his opponent's rhythm illustrates the importance of adaptability and tactical thinking in competitive sports.

Lesson: Analyze your opponents' weaknesses and adjust your game plan to gain the upper hand.

- **Believe in Yourself:** Despite falling behind in the match, Nadal never lost faith in his ability to mount a comeback. His stunning performance is a testament to the power of never giving up, no matter how hopeless the situation may seem.

Lesson: Maintain belief, stay disciplined, and have confidence in your ability. Success often requires persistence, grit, and tenacity, even when the odds are stacked against you.

CELEBRATING SUCCESS AND LEARNING FROM LOSS

Whether you win or lose, you can always learn from the experience. Winning is fantastic, and you should take the time to celebrate. Remember though, even when you win there are always areas where you can become even better.

Losing is not the end of the world. View it as a chance to figure out what went wrong and how you can improve. Take some time after the game to reflect on how you did. What did you do well, and what can you do better? Did you pull off that skill you've been working on at training? How was your footwork? And what about your mental game? Were you able to apply the strategies you've been working on in your mental skills sessions?

By breaking down your performance like this, you can figure out where to focus your efforts during training and keep improving.

Handling Winning and Losing With Grace and Humility

Winning is fantastic, but it doesn't mean you're better than anyone else. Be thankful for your teammates, coaches, and opponents—they all play a part in your success. And instead of getting comfy and thinking you've made it, keep pushing yourself to improve. There's always something new to learn and ways to grow, even when you're at the top of your game.

Losing sucks. But it's how you bounce back that really matters. Take some time to feel disappointed, but don't dwell on it for too long. Instead, use that feeling to fuel your determination to do better next time. Think about what you could have done differently and how you can turn that loss into a lesson. Remember, setbacks don't define you—they make you stronger and more resilient for the challenges that lay ahead. So keep your head up, keep working hard, and get ready to boss it next time!

CHAPTER FOUR: THREE KEY POINTS I NEED TO WORK ON

I Need To:

1. _____

2. _____

3. _____

How I'll Do It:

1. _____

2. _____

3. _____

When I'll Check My Progress:

1. _____

2. _____

3. _____

FIVE
OVERCOMING FEARS AND ANXIETY

Anxiety is an overwhelming feeling of fear-worrying stress. It often affects athletes before a competition. As we've already discussed, it's normal to have a certain amount of anxiety before you perform. And it doesn't matter how often you've done something—the anxiety remains.

Think of your favorite YouTuber. I'll bet that in the moments before they go live, they experience butterflies in their stomach or a slightly dry throat as the physical effects of anxiety kick in.

This anxiety level is good because it helps them take the task seriously and perform well. It's the same thing with sporting competition. A controlled level of anxiety causes your body to produce more of the hormones that make you feel energized and increase your pain tolerance.

But it's all too easy to let your pregame anxiety spiral out of control. When it does, your ability to focus and perform goes out the window. In this chapter, we'll explore a range of strategies to help you keep your pregame anxiety under control so that, even though you've got butterflies in your stomach, they're all flying in formation.

STRATEGIES TO OVERCOME FEAR AND ANXIETY

Fear is a normal and healthy reaction that warns our bodies to be careful. Anxiety is a type of fear that involves more worry about what may go wrong in the future than fear of something in the present.

When you become fearful, your focus changes. Rather than focusing on the task at hand, you let your thoughts and emotions distract you. Your fear paralyzes you, preventing your natural talents and trained skills from showing themselves. You'll likely find it difficult to get better during competition, which can feed your fear and anxiety even further.

The following is a five-step strategy for overcoming fear and anxiety:

Step One: Identify Your Triggers

Awareness is the first step to overcoming fear and anxiety. It's like shining a light on the shadows—they can't scare you when you can see them. By becoming aware of what triggers your anxiety, you gain the power to tackle it head-on.

Think about those big moments, like grand final matches, or taking a penalty kick that could win your team the game. Just knowing that all eyes are on you can get your heart racing and your palms sweaty. And then there's the fear of getting injured, which can hang over you like a dark cloud, especially if you've been hurt before.

But anxiety triggers aren't one-size-fits-all. What sets one person off might not bother someone else at all. That's why it's essential to identify what causes your own personal anxiety.

Take some time to write down your thoughts and feelings before, during, and after games or practices. This is where keeping a journal can again be of benefit. Notice any patterns or recurring themes—these could be clues to what's really getting under your skin, helping you better identify and develop strategies for managing them.

It's also important to consider the role of past experiences in shaping your anxiety triggers. Maybe you've had a bad game or suffered an injury in the past, and now you're worried it'll happen again. These negative experiences can create a kind of mental baggage that weighs you down, making it harder to stay calm and focused on the present.

But here's the thing: just because something happened in the past, doesn't mean it has to dictate your future. By acknowledging how past experiences have shaped your anxiety triggers, you can start to work through them and move forward with confidence.

Step Two: Reframe the Situation

Let's rewind to 2008 and check out Tiger Woods at the U.S. Golf Open. He was dealing with some serious physical problems—like a double stress fracture and a torn ACL—but he kept it all under wraps. Even though he was hurting, he managed to push through and make it to the final round.

Picture this: Tiger's in a sudden-death playoff, and the pressure is unbelievable. A reporter asks him if he felt the weight of making this epic comeback. Tiger's response? He admitted he was nervous but said that's actually a good thing. He explained feeling nervous means you care, and that you can use this energy to better your focus and rise to the challenge.

So, what's Tiger talking about? As mentioned in Chapter Four, it's called **reframing**. Instead of seeing those pregame jitters as bad, you look at them differently. Some people crumble under pressure because they think all those nerves are a sign of something negative. But others, like Tiger, see it as a chance to step up.

Here's the cool part: those butterflies in your stomach and that racing heart? They're your body's way of preparing for action. So, the next time you're feeling those pregame nerves, remember Tiger's advice: don't try to get rid of them—use them! See them as a sign that you care about your performance and you're ready to tackle whatever comes your way. It's all about changing how you think about those feelings and turning them into fuel for success.

Step Three: Detachment

Kevin De Bruyne is a championship winning midfielder for Manchester City FC. Prior to taking the field, he uses detachment as a pregame strategy to calm his nerves. He is well known for playing Candy Crush on his phone as all the nervous tension is building around him. Kevin says, "I just play games and talk to people…The more relaxed I am before, the better I feel."

Detachment means taking a step back from all that pressure. Instead of letting it overwhelm you, find something fun or relaxing to do. Whether listening to music or playing games, do whatever helps you unwind.

Detachment is an intelligent way to handle those big-game nerves. And you don't have to do it on your own. Teams can do it together too. Before a big game, you might play card games or goof around as one. It can help you bond and keep everyone calm.

But here's the thing: when it's game time, you've got to switch gears. That means turning your focus to preparing to smash it out on the court or field. It's all about balancing the time to chill out and bringing your A-game when it counts.

Remember your pregame routine and rituals that we discussed in the last chapter? These will help you transition from detachment to focus. One vital aspect of the pregame routine is that it is very familiar to you. This provides you with a sense of control. The more in control you feel, the less fearful and anxious you'll be.

So, the next time you feel those pregame jitters, remember De Bruyne's trick: detach, chill out, and then show them what you've got when it matters most!

Step Four: Minimize Fear of the Unknown

Performance anxiety can be caused by fear of the unknown. Let's say you're competing in a tournament. The setting is bigger, the surroundings are different, and there are way more people.

We can call these things unknown variables. A key to controlling performance anxiety is to focus on the known variables. These include your training and preparation. Constantly remind yourself that you've done all the preparation work and are prepared for what lies ahead. You know your teammates, you've done your homework on the opposition, and you have complete trust in your coach.

A second step is to reduce the number of unknown variables. So, perhaps you get to the competition venue an hour or so early to familiarize yourself with the facilities. Check out the change rooms, as well as the layout of the field, court, or track. Visualize yourself performing confidently in that space, making it feel more familiar and less intimidating.

Step Five: Performance Goal Setting

Performance goal setting adds an extra step to the positive reframing we discussed earlier and can help you address the things you're worried about failing at. For example, suppose your problem area is the basketball free throw. In that case, your performance goal might be to improve your free throw accuracy by making at least 8 out of 10 shots during practice sessions this week.

Then, during the game, knowing you've practiced your free throws all week will help alleviate any anxiety you may have surrounding this aspect of your performance. Just imagine you are practicing your free throws again at training. Instead of letting fear take over, you channel your energy into working toward achieving the goal you set yourself through the week. This not only helps to distract your mind from negative thoughts but also gives you a sense of purpose and direction.

EXTERNAL PRESSURES

External pressures are the kind that come from outside of yourself. They might include pressures from parents, coaches, and even social media. Let's explore the most common external pressures youth athletes face and strategies for dealing with them.

Expectations from Coaches: Your coach wants you to succeed, but sometimes it might feel like they are putting too much pressure on you. It may be that your coach wants to win a specific title or encourages you to play a bit more aggressively against a rival opponent (like in a derby match). Additionally, they may focus heavily on specific performance targets, such as achieving personal best times, scoring a certain number of goals, or covering set running distances during a game. This pressure to perform can be stressful, especially in team sports where failing to meet these expectations could result in being left out of the starting lineup or substituted off if your coach feels your performance is lacking.

Expectations from Parents: Your parents love you and want to see you do your best in sports. But sometimes, they might have high hopes for you, which can feel like a lot of pressure. It could be that your mom or dad played a specific sport, were quite successful, and would love to see you achieve the same. Or maybe you have participated in the same sport they did, but now you would rather play something else. Perhaps they want you to gain a sports scholarship or play for a particular team. Despite their best intentions, these expectations can sometimes be stressful if your goals don't align with theirs.

Social Media Pressure: Social media can be fun but also make you feel like you've always got to be perfect. Seeing other athletes post about their successes might make you feel like you're not good enough and leave you constantly comparing yourself to your teammates or opposition. You may also feel pressured to post content that shows off your athletic skills or helps you to maintain a particular image or persona. When these posts or reels don't receive the number of views, likes, or comments you are hoping for, it can also negatively impact your confidence. Finally, social media can be a considerable source of distraction. It can lead to procrastination and reduce time spent on important tasks like training and academic responsibilities.

Expectations from Your Teammates: Your teammates can also add to your stress levels. They might expect you to perform at a certain level or be disappointed if you don't play as well as they had hoped. It could be that during a match you do not execute your role as effectively as needed, and this can lead to outbursts of frustration and disharmony.

Scouts & Talent Identification: When trialing for a new team, you often only get a limited amount of time to make a good first impression and showcase your talent. Not only are you competing, but so are many other athletes who may be trialing for the same position on the team that you are. This can be somewhat stressful as you must perform and do your best to impress in a relatively short period of time.

The same is true when scouts are present during a game. This can be quite daunting, especially if they are there specifically to watch you play and evaluate your potential for a scholarship or to be drafted into a competition.

STRATEGIES TO DEAL WITH EXTERNAL PRESSURE

Now that we've identified sources of external pressure let's explore ways to manage expectations and reduce the overall stress associated with these situations.

Open Communication: If you're feeling overwhelmed by pressure from coaches, parents, or teammates, remember that you have the power to address it. It is essential to talk about how you're feeling and discuss ways that they can best support you. It's alright to say no or tell someone when they put too much pressure on you. Practice speaking up for yourself in a kind but firm way, and remember that taking care of yourself first is not just okay, it's necessary for your well-being.

Identify Your Priorities: Reflect on what matters most to you in sports and life. Writing these priorities down can also be a simple way for you to visualize where to direct your time and energy and establish limits for things of lesser importance.

Limit Social Media: If the pressure of social media is negatively impacting your self image and performance as an athlete, you may want to consider limiting the amount of time you spend scrolling or posting content. While having a social media presence as an athlete can be beneficial, it should not add to the stressors you already have to contend with.

Pay No Attention: Unless you are required to, do not pay attention to scouts or coaches who you know are at an event watching you perform. Treat the tryout or match like you would any other training session or competition, complete with all your normal routines and a positive mindset.

Professional Support: If you are overwhelmed by pressure and unsure how to cope, remember that it's perfectly okay to seek help. A sports psychologist or counselor can equip you with the tools and strategies needed to manage your stress and build resilience. Don't hesitate to reach out if you need assistance.

BUILDING CONFIDENCE AFTER A SETBACK

Setbacks can be really tough, especially when you're closing in on a goal. You may have trained hard all preseason, achieved all your technique goals, and even celebrated winning a championship title with your team. However, despite your best efforts when trialing for a representative squad, you still didn't make the cut.

Feeling shocked, upset, or angry is normal. But ignoring these feelings won't make them go away. Instead, try to acknowledge and express your emotions in a healthy way. Bottling them up will only make things more challenging in the long run.

If you develop the right mentality, you can always find positives. It's all about having that growth mindset we discussed in Chapter One and asking yourself, "What can I learn from this situation? Is there anything I could have done better?"

Remember, setbacks are not a measure of your worth or potential. It's just an opportunity to identify areas for improvement and grow!

STEPS TO RECOVERY

If your confidence has taken a hit after a setback, here are a few steps you can follow to mentally help get you back on track:

Reflection: Recovering from a setback takes time and patience. Start by reflecting on possible contributing factors. These could include a lack of pregame physical and mental preparation, weather conditions, poor decision-making or technical ability, and opponent skill level. If video footage is available, it can be an extremely beneficial tool in helping you analyze your performance to see where improvements can be made.

Compassion: Practice self-compassion and remember that everyone faces setbacks. Being kind to yourself is critical, particularly when a setback results from factors outside of your control. Treat yourself like you would a teammate who's struggling. Instead of criticizing, offer support and encouragement.

Review Past Successes: Again, if you can access video footage, review matches or highlight reels of your previous successful performances. Alternatively, using the PETTLEP visualization technique discussed in Chapter Two can allow you to fully immerse yourself in what past successes felt like. These two strategies can be a fantastic reminder of what you are capable of to help you regain your confidence.

Letting Go: The world's best athletes are great at this. Yes, it's natural to feel disappointed but do not let a setback get the best of you. If you have identified areas for improvement, set new goals, and are focused on bettering your performance next time, let it go, move forward, and start paving the way for your future success.

PARENT'S CORNER: LEARNING FROM SETBACKS

Your child's response to setbacks is often influenced by the example you provide. If your child makes a mistake during a game or doesn't make a specific team, don't try to buffer them by blaming someone else, like the referee, coach, or scout. Instead, teach your child to take responsibility for what happened and help them identify the skills they need to develop. Once these areas are identified, work together to set a goal for improvement.

If you're watching your child compete and they genuinely get a bad call from the referee, don't make an issue of it. Instead, encourage your child to put it behind them and focus on the next play rather than dwelling on the foul call.

Look out, too, for positive role models who overcome setbacks with grace and dignity. You might spot this in a post-match interview on TV when a losing athlete acknowledges their playing errors and commits to coming back better. Point these examples out to your child as examples of a growth mindset.

COMING BACK FROM AN INJURY

Unfortunately, sustaining an injury of some kind throughout your athletic career can be the price you pay for participating in the sport you love. When it does occur, your body needs time to heal, whether it be for a short while or even a whole season. This can understandably leave you feeling devastated and disconnected from something that brings you joy and purpose.

Coming back from an injury isn't just about getting your body back in shape; it's also about taking care of your mind. One big challenge is a lack of confidence when you get back out there. This can make you hold back during games and play more cautiously.

Lack of confidence however may not be the only emotion you'll experience as you recover. Anger, disappointment, impatience, and uncertainty may also haunt you.

Here are five strategies that will help you get through this tough time and come back to your sport feeling mentally stronger:

- **Set realistic goals:** Instead of focusing on the end goal of being fully recovered, break it down into smaller, achievable goals. Whether regaining strength, improving flexibility, or mastering a new skill, setting smaller goals will help you stay motivated and track your progress. You may also use this recovery time to focus on developing your understanding of tactical elements of the game, or building strength through a weaker limb. Try to focus on your progress no matter how small. Celebrate every little victory along the way!
- **Visualize success:** Spend time visualizing yourself back on the field, doing what you love injury free and fully recovered. Picture yourself playing confidently and performing at your best. This can help build your confidence and self-belief.
- **Stay connected:** Don't isolate yourself during your recovery. If you're able to, still attend team training and game days. Staying connected with your teammates, coaches, and friends is crucial during this tough time. They can provide support, encouragement, and a sense of belonging. As your recovery progresses, you may also be able to commence a modified training program. This could include performing running drills on the same field as your teammates or participating in some aspects of team training such as the warm up or isolated technical skills.
- **Talk about your feelings:** Feeling frustrated or anxious about your injury is okay. Talk to your parents, coach or friends

about your feelings. Sharing your emotions can help lighten the load and make you feel less alone.
- **Focus on what you can control:** While you can't go back and change that you got injured, you can control how you respond. Focus on your attitude, effort, and dedication to your recovery. You'll return physically and mentally stronger by putting in the work and staying committed.

PARENT'S CORNER: INJURIES

Having an injured child with athletic talent can be hard on both of you, but your support can make a world of difference to their recovery. Here are some ways you can help your child navigate this challenging time:

- **Be patient and understanding:** Understand that your child may feel frustrated, disappointed, or even scared about their injury and return to sport. Be patient as they navigate these emotions, and actively listen to their concerns without judgment. Let them know that their feelings are valid and you support them no matter what.
- **Provide practical support:** Help your child with practical tasks related to their injury. This can include scheduling doctor's appointments, attending physical therapy sessions, or assisting with exercises and rehabilitation at home. Your involvement shows them that you're invested in their recovery and well-being. This can help boost their morale, knowing they have a strong support system behind them every step of the way.
- **Stay positive and optimistic:** Be a source of positivity and encouragement for your child. Celebrate their progress, no matter how small, and remind them that setbacks are a normal part of recovery. Help them focus on the future and the goals they can achieve once they've fully healed.
- **Be their advocate:** Advocate for your child's needs, whether it's communicating with their coaches about modified training

plans, ensuring they have access to necessary medical care, or advocating for them if they encounter any challenges or obstacles during their recovery.
- **Lead by example:** Show your child how to approach challenges with resilience and determination through leading by example. Let them see you staying positive, adapting to setbacks, and supporting them wholeheartedly through the ups and downs of their recovery journey.

CHAPTER FIVE: THREE KEY POINTS I NEED TO WORK ON

I Need To:

1. _____
2. _____
3. _____

How I'll Do It:

1. _____
2. _____
3. _____

When I'll Check My Progress:

1. _____
2. _____
3. _____

CASE STUDY ONE: FROM THE SIDELINES TO CENTER COURT - RUBEN BORG'S STORY

I can't relate to lazy people. We don't speak the same language. I don't understand you. I don't want to understand you.—Kobe Bryant

Ruben's basketball journey began when he was 14 years old. Initially, he found it difficult to make it into higher level teams with some significant growth spurts temporarily affecting his coordination and leading to several injury concerns. Regardless of these challenges, Ruben refused to be defeated. Instead, he embarked on a rigorous training regimen, performing morning gym sessions with me before school and then honing his basketball skills in the afternoon and late into the evening through his team practice, one-on-one coaching sessions, and countless hours of individual technical work.

After a year characterized by relentless grit and determination, Ruben began to attract attention, earning sought-after positions on academy and state representative teams. His talents did not go unnoticed internationally either; an invitation from a US-based scouting agency saw him tour the United States in 2022. During this time, Ruben showcased his prowess on the court in a number of tournaments where scouts from high schools and colleges alike were in attendance.

Following the tour, Ruben's efforts were rewarded with multiple scholarship offers from American schools, one of which he warmly accepted in North Carolina. So, at 16 years of age, he undertook the bold move of relocating from Australia to the United States on his own, immersing himself in campus life at his new high school. Two years on, Ruben continues to excel not only with his basketball but also academically ... his achievements serving as a testament to his dedication and the belief that no dream is too big when pursued with passion and determination.

CAROL: Ruben, you packed up and moved to the US when you were only 16. It takes a lot of courage and resilience to do that at such a young age. What thought processes helped you get there and manage such a big change?

RUBEN: I would say, first of all, I didn't want to do it; my dad however said to me a year before I came here, "You might have to go over to the States." But I was like, "That's such a big thing to do at such a young age." Then, I honestly just realized that if I wanted to chase my dreams and achieve my goals, the best place to do that was overseas. I knew the earlier I got over here, the better it was going to be for me to develop and become the player that I need to be ... to make it to where I want to be. I felt like I wasn't getting that back home in Australia. There is just more opportunities and growth available for me here in the States.

CAROL: Once you did move over, did you struggle to fit in initially with your teammates and find your position within the team?

RUBEN: I'm pretty good at meeting new people. It's something I'm comfortable with, so regardless of where I'm from, it wasn't a struggle.

Having an Australian accent also helped because people were like, "Oh, you're an Australian!" and everyone wants to talk to you.

When I think of my teammates, basically everyone was from somewhere around the world, not just from America. There were Americans, but most of us were international students … so I feel like we bonded over that. We connected on things like moving away from home and not having family around. So, in a sense, we became a family together.

CAROL: I know you suffered a significant injury to your wrist, which only happened a couple of weeks after being in the USA. How did you feel initially? What were your thought processes afterward that helped manage your recovery?

RUBEN: So initially, I was really upset. I was right-hand dominant, and that's the one I broke. I came here to play basketball, and then, all of a sudden, I couldn't play. So I was annoyed at the start, but then I realized God did it for a reason … I'm realizing that now, there was other stuff I needed to work on.

I could use my left hand and my legs, so I was in the gym on the Vertimax jumping and just doing everything I could do with my left hand that I couldn't do with my right. I felt like just being in the weight room and gym every single day, dribbling with my left, and doing defensive work really built my resilience and my character. I know not everyone would have done that if they had a broken wrist.

But that's not how I function … I can't be lazy. I would have just beat myself up if I were being lazy. Especially considering the opportunity I've been given. So when something like that happens to me, the best thing I can do is to be positive and keep pursuing all the aspects of my game that I know I can improve. I can't just dwell on the negative.

CAROL: Has there been a moment during a game when you had to rely on mental resilience to get you through it? And what was the outcome of that?

RUBEN: I'll give you a little flashback to last year and my game-winning layup. It was in the season playoffs. We played a school we had beat twice before, but I was having a pretty off performance. My coach, however, was still giving me plenty of game time.

Photo Credit: Tyler Goddard

The score was 46-46 ... and leading up to the game, there was a lot of trash-talking from the other school. So I went into the match with the mindset that I wasn't going to let anyone beat me in anything because they can't talk to me that way.

Photo Credit: Recruiting Boost (International Camp 2022)

Anyway, their team was in possession at the top of the key, but I managed to steal the ball and dribble it down the court with 3 or 4 seconds left on the clock. Then, right before the buzzer, I did a left-handed layup, and it went in. And I felt like if I hadn't broken my right wrist earlier in the year, would I have made that left-hand shot? I don't know.

At that moment, though, I felt like I wasn't really thinking much ... had I been thinking too hard, I reckon I probably would have missed the shot. I would have overthought it, so I just had to rely on my training.

I still felt like that game was pretty tough for me though, because mentally, I hadn't really been checked in ... leading up to that point I had made a lot of mistakes and missed shots, but in that critical moment I just let my skill and my hard work shine through me, and God, obviously.

CAROL: Before a game, is there anything you do to get yourself mentally prepared? Is there a routine or something you do to get yourself into the zone?

RUBEN: I mean, I've got a lot of superstitions, even though I try to limit them.

CAROL: Can you tell me what a few of those superstitions are?

RUBEN: Well, I still tape my wrist basically before every game. I write down what my goals are for the game and what I'm grateful for—whether that be God, family, or what I want to achieve for the match.

Also whenever I take my chain off, it's a cross, I put it in one of the crocs (shoes) that I wear which also has my favorite number (3) on it. I do that every single time. I also like listening to my favorite singer, J. Cole, before games and saying a prayer before taking the court. That's all my superstitions, and, oh yeah ... I've been doing a lot more journaling and goal setting lately, which has really helped me perform for games.

CAROL: So, from a resilience point of view, what do you need to work on? Is there anything that you find difficult to deal with, like criticism or fear of failure?

RUBEN: I would say the most difficult thing is comparing myself to others and my self-belief. I work extremely hard—you know this—but having self-belief is tough sometimes. I've been getting better at it though, by setting goals and practicing gratitude every morning. It's really helping me to believe in my ability.

And when it comes to comparing myself to other people, there's really no point. That's what I try to tell myself. I feel like everyone does that though in anything; whether you have a normal job or are a professional athlete, you're gonna compare things like … "Am I as good as this player?" … "Can I do what they do?" But I think it's just a waste of time. Everyone's different. No one person on this earth is remotely close to who you are. So, having self-belief, having confidence in yourself and your skills, and not trying to compare your journey to someone else's is really important … especially in sports.

With regards to criticism and having other people trying to get in my head, I don't really have a mind for that. It doesn't really affect me … if anything, it actually kind of helps. It makes me think, "Well, okay, you've worked on that." so there's no need for you to believe what they're saying.

CAROL: So, if anything else, it fuels you.

RUBEN: Yeah, absolutely.

CAROL: Do you believe that mental toughness can be worked on and improved over time? If so, how have you done that?

RUBEN: Of course, one hundred percent! … I've done it through journaling … but it also comes through experience and practice as well. I mean, I know some people who don't seem to work on the mental side of the game, but they're really good basketball players. I think they have just developed their resilience over a long period of time. On the other hand, I know players who struggle with a lot of mental cloudiness, but they work on it and challenge their thinking every day.

Putting in that effort helps improve their resilience. It can definitely be taught and developed. It can also come more naturally to some more than others; everyone's different.

Photo Credit: Caleb Gravley (@cajo.media)

CAROL: From a resilience point of view, do you have a favorite player that you admire for their mental toughness and ability?

RUBEN: Yeah, Kobe Bryant, one hundred percent. When I was back home, I was listening to Kobe every day. I mean, his stories are just really inspiring. I love how everyone would talk about him—about how he would be in the gym before everyone else was there, how he would work his arse off all the time.

Photo Credit: Kasia Sutton

I respect the way he would come out and just have that mindset.

Of course, Kobe was an NBA player and an absolute great, but he wasn't always like that. He had to work for what he got, and he used to tell stories about all that stuff. I just find it motivating because I aspire to be like him by working really hard and doing what I can with what I've been given. For example, I'm doing this interview in the weight room at my school; it's 9:30 p.m. on a Friday night, and I've just finished a workout. So I'm taking advantage of what I have and the facilities I have access to, and that's what Kobe did.

CAROL: Lastly, do you have a favorite quote, saying, or song lyric that inspires you? That encapsulates your journey and what you want to achieve as an athlete and basketball player?

RUBEN: Yeah, of course. It's a song by J. Cole called "Sideline Story." And it's about how to get off the sidelines, using basketball as a reference, but he's talking about life in general as well. In the song, he said he wishes somebody had made guidelines on how to make it off the sidelines. He talks about how he wants the whole world to know who he is, and it's just very inspiring because I want that same stuff. I want the entire world to know my name. I want them to know what I've been through, and he basically speaks for me in that song; it's just very relatable. So whenever I need it, I listen to it.

To watch Ruben in action scan the QR below to be taken to his YouTube channel.

SIX
HANDLING CRITICISM AND FEEDBACK

It is normal to enjoy praise and dislike criticism. True character is when you prevent either from affecting you in a negative matter.
– John Wooden

Imagine you're out there, giving it your all. You've got the ball, and you're feeling good. You know you can make a drive toward the goal. But then you hear it—the sharp voice of your coach booming from the sidelines: "Pass the ball!"

Your heart sinks as you feel the weight of that criticism. In an instant, your positive feelings evaporate to be replaced by feelings of frustration and negativity. You've lost focus. The opposing player pounces, and you lose the ball. Then, to make things worse, you hear a groan from your coach on the sidelines.

Criticism can be tough to take, especially when it's hurled at you in the middle of a game. However, it is just as natural to athletic competition as the crowd's roar, or the thrill of victory. Learning how to handle criticism and feedback constructively is critical to your success as an athlete. Just like learning to perfect your shot or mastering a new move, developing resilience in the face of criticism is a skill that can take your game to the next level. So, instead of letting criticism knock you down, let's explore how to use it as a stepping stone toward becoming the best athlete—and person—you can be.

CONSTRUCTIVE CRITICISM VS. NEGATIVE FEEDBACK

The first step in handling feedback is to sort out the good feedback from the bad feedback. Constructive criticism aims to help you improve. It's specific, actionable, and focused on behaviors rather than personal attributes.

Negative feedback is the opposite: it's vague, unhelpful, and often designed to tear you down rather than build you up.

Here are contrasting examples to illustrate the difference. This feedback is given to a soccer player who is not passing the ball enough:

Constructive Criticism

- "Hey, during the game, I noticed a few opportunities where you could have passed to a teammate in a better position. Consider scanning the field more often to find those passing lanes."
- "I've noticed that you sometimes hold onto the ball for too long. Remember, soccer is a team sport, and passing is crucial for creating scoring opportunities. Try to be more aware of your teammates' positions and look for passing options sooner.

Negative Feedback

- "You're not the only player on the team! Stop being so selfish out there and pass the ball."
- "Why do you always hog the ball? You're never going to improve if you keep playing like that."

HOW TO HANDLE NEGATIVE FEEDBACK

Negative feedback is not helpful. In a perfect world, you wouldn't receive it at all. But unfortunately, you'll likely come up against it from time to time.

Here are six strategies to help you deal with this type of harsh criticism:

1. Stay Calm and Resilient: When receiving negative feedback, it's natural to feel defensive or upset. This is where resilience comes in. You can't control what others say to you, but you can control how it affects you. Whether you allow it to crush you or pass you by is a choice.

Discipline yourself to stay calm and objective. Take a deep breath and remind yourself that feedback can be helpful, even if it is poorly delivered.

2. Focus on the Message, Not the Delivery: Instead of dwelling on the feedback's delivery, focus on the underlying message. Look for any valuable nuggets of information that you can use to improve your performance. For example, in the last section, the underlying message is that you must pass the ball more—nothing more, nothing less. Take that away and forget the rest.

3. Seek Clarification: If the negative feedback is vague or unclear, ask for clarification. Politely ask the person providing the feedback to elaborate on their point of view or provide specific examples. This can help you better understand their criticism and devise a plan to improve.

4. Maintain Perspective: Remember that negative feedback is just one person's opinion. It doesn't define your worth as an athlete. Keep things in perspective, and don't let it shake your confidence. Focus on your strengths and the progress you've made rather than dwelling on criticism.

5. Seek Support: Don't hesitate to seek support from teammates, coaches, or trusted mentors when dealing with negative feedback. They can offer perspective, encouragement, and constructive advice to help you navigate challenging situations.

6. Turn a Negative Into a Positive: Use negative feedback as motivation to prove any critics wrong. Channel frustration or disappointment into fuel for improvement. Let it drive you to work harder and strive for excellence on the field.

This is exactly what four-time NBA champion and two-time MVP, Stephen Curry has done numerous times throughout his career:

STEPHEN CURRY'S SUPERPOWER

Watch the NBA's Golden State Warriors superstar on court, and everything seems effortless. Yet, despite his fantastic talent and strong work ethic, Stephen Curry has faced many challenges on his journey to greatness.

As a teenager, Curry was often overlooked by coaches because of his small stature. He was also perceived to be not very athletic. For these reasons, he missed out on offers from several major conference colleges, including Duke University.

However Stephen refused to let these setbacks discourage him. Instead, he used them as motivation to prove his doubters wrong. He worked harder than ever to improve his skills, strengthen his body, and perfect his game.

During the summer before his second year of high school, Curry worked hard to improve his shooting technique. He spent countless hours practicing with his dad, Dell. They focused on where he let go of the ball and how he finished his shot. By paying close attention to how he shot the ball when he was young, Curry set himself up for immense success in the NBA.

Stephen credits his resilience (which he has called his superpower), to being the driving force that has propelled him to become one of the greatest shooters the game has ever seen.

In an inspirational video that went viral, Stephen demonstrates this superpower when he was given his NBA pre-draft scout report to read. This is what the report said:

> *Far below NBA standard with regards to explosiveness, and athleticism...at six-two he is extremely small for the NBA shooting guard position, and would likely keep him from being much of a defender at the next level. Struggles defensively getting around screens, can overshoot, and rush into shots from time to time. Needs to add some muscle to his upper body, but appears as though he will always be skinny...*

After reading the report aloud, what was Stephen's response you may ask? In a humble, yet motivating display of how to handle criticism Stephen replied with:

> *"I'd just like to say I appreciate all the motivation and inspiration to do everything this paper said I couldn't do."*

...Well said Stephen!

DEBRIEFING

Discussing what happened during your performance is a vital aspect of the competitive process that you must go through before moving on. It's called debriefing.

Whether you win or lose, you can always learn from your performance. The debrief is where you identify possible areas for improvement and start setting goals. It's easy to put the game behind you (especially when you lose), but this post-performance analysis is a habit that will set you and your team apart as athletes. And, as you know, it's the small habits that make all the difference.

Two types of debriefing should ideally take place. These include:

The Immediate Debrief

Debriefing with your team directly after a game is crucial for several reasons. Firstly, it allows you, your teammates, and your coach the chance to express any raw, unfiltered emotions and insights while the performance is still fresh in your mind. This immediate reflection can help identify strengths and any areas for improvement in the performance, enabling everyone to acknowledge what worked well and what didn't.

Secondly, when done right, it encourages a sense of unity and joint responsibility, as every team member has the chance to voice their experiences and perspectives. This can be of considerable benefit in building team cohesion and ensuring that any frustrations or mistakes are dealt with promptly, reducing the risk of issues festering until the next training session.

The Training Debrief

The first session back at training is where a more detailed debrief can take place. As initial emotions have subsided, a greater emphasis can be placed on a more objective analysis of individual and team performances.

Your coach has often had the time needed to review notes or game footage and formulate a structured debrief. Here, key moments of the performance can be analyzed and discussed amongst the team. This can include not only your own team's tactics and decisions, but also those of the opposing team and how it may have influenced your team's performance.

The training debrief additionally allows you and your coach to have a more in depth one-on-one discussion about your individual performance. Topics of discussion here may include where you excelled, or areas that technically and tactically you need to work on. Remember that this conversation doesn't necessarily have to be initiated by your coach. For the sake of your development as an athlete, it is okay to make the first move and actively seek your coach's feedback.

The only thing to remember when going into this conversation is to keep an open mind and be willing to take on board any criticism.

COACHES CORNER: DEBRIEFING

Both debriefing strategies mentioned above can be incredibly beneficial in reinforcing lessons learned, establishing goals, and helping you plan future training sessions for your team. They can also encourage a continuous learning environment in which you and your athletes constantly evolve and adapt based on recent experiences.

Unfortunately however, I have seen some coaches manage this important post-performance discussion quite poorly—particularly when it comes to the immediate debrief following a loss.

As a coach, you are highly invested in how your team performs. A defeat can leave you feeling just as upset, frustrated, and disappointed as your young athletes. However, how you respond in those critical moments following the game can heavily influence your team's morale.

Here are some things to keep in mind heading into this debrief:

- **Remember You Are a Role Model:** As a coach, you are a leader and a role model. Your young athletes look to you for guidance, support and to set a good example. Remember this before formulating any sort of response and addressing your team.
- **Keep Calm:** As disheartening as a loss may be, keep your emotions in check. If needed, take a few minutes to gather your thoughts and let your emotions settle.
- **Don't Lay Blame:** One of the worst things you can do during this debrief is to start negatively singling out players. If costly individual errors have been made, it is likely that these players will already be acutely aware of their mistakes. Now is not the time to make this a focus of discussion. Give yourself and your athletes time to calm down before addressing individual errors.
- **Manage the Discussion:** Should talk amongst teammates get heated, and negative emotions start taking over, take control of the situation. Do what you can to return the conversation back to where constructive criticism is the goal.
- **Look for Positives:** Try to find silver linings in your team's performance to help boost morale. Although you did not win the game, it could be that your team did not concede any goals in the second half, or perhaps they reduced the points deficit. Regardless of the end result, if there are any positives that can be taken away be sure to acknowledge them.
- **Postpone the Debrief:** If you find that despite your best efforts, you are still struggling to keep any negative emotions in check, the best thing may be to postpone further discussions until the next training session. Instead of addressing your team and risking saying something you may regret, quickly take the time to inform your athletes that you would rather discuss the performance at a later date. Do not, however, make this a habit. Remember that this is a time of need when your players will still look to you for inspiration and guidance.

DIFFICULT CONVERSATIONS WITH COACHES AND TEAMMATES

As mentioned in Chapter Four, communicating openly and honestly with your coaches and teammates builds trust, understanding, and support. You learn from each other, lift each other up, and work together to reach your goals. It creates an atmosphere where you feel valued and confident, fostering personal growth and leading to better individual and team performances.

Good communication skills can also be an incredibly powerful tool when approaching difficult conversations with your coach and teammates.

Here are some tips to help you effectively express your needs or concerns when issues arise:

Tip #1: Choose the Right Time and Place: Don't bring up sensitive topics during heated moments or in front of others. Instead, wait for the right time and place where you can speak openly and without distractions.

Tip #2: Be Clear and Specific: Clearly state your needs or concerns. Use specific examples to illustrate your point. Don't use vague or generalized language that may lead to misunderstandings.

Tip #3: Use "I" Statements: Use "I" language to take ownership of your feelings and experiences. For example, instead of saying, "You always ignore me during practice," say, "I feel frustrated when I don't receive feedback." This helps avoid placing blame and encourages constructive conversation.

Tip #4: Keep Your Emotions in Check: If you are discussing an issue of concern, where perhaps you feel wrongly done by, do your best to keep your emotions in check. Stick to the facts, and don't let your negative emotions overwhelm you. This can help avoid saying something that you may later regret.

Tip #5: Actively Listen: Effective communication is a two-way street. Listen carefully to your coaches' or teammates' responses without interrupting. Show empathy and understanding by acknowledging their point of view, even if you disagree. Repeat back what you've heard to ensure you understand each other correctly.

Tip #6: Seek Solutions Together: Go into the conversation with a collaborative mindset. Working together to find solutions encourages teamwork and strengthens relationships.

Tip #7: Respect Boundaries: Respect your coaches' and teammates' boundaries, just as you expect them to respect yours. Be aware of their time, energy, and personal space. Don't pressure them to deal with your concerns immediately. Give them time to process the conversation and respond when they are ready.

CHAPTER SIX: THREE KEY POINTS I NEED TO WORK ON

I Need To:

1. _____
2. _____
3. _____

How I'll Do It:

1. _____
2. _____
3. _____

When I'll Check My Progress:

1. _____
2. _____
3. _____

CASE STUDY TWO: LOCAL TALENT TO INTERNATIONAL SUCCESS - KAI CALDERBANK-PARK'S JOURNEY

It is part of being a goalkeeper: there is nobody behind to save you.
— Hugo Lloris

I had the privilege of working with Kai in 2015 and 2016 when he was just 15. Playing for the Wollongong Wolves (the "South Coast Wolves" at the time), we won the New South Wales State NPL1 Championship in 2015. At the end of the 2016 season, Kai headed to the UK to trial for several English Premier League youth academies.

One of the clubs Kai trialed for was Burnley FC, who liked the young Aussie's style and offered Kai a two-year contract. Since then, Kai has lived the life of a professional footballer in the UK. During this time, he has played for a number of clubs across England and Wales. Most notably of late, Kai was a part of the 2023 championship-winning team at Wrexham FC, owned by none other than actors Ryan Reynolds and

Rob McElhenney. Kai even appeared in episodes of "Welcome to Wrexham," the recent Disney+ documentary series.

Over the years, Kai's talent has also been acknowledged internationally, with his selection for both the Under 19s and Under 23s Australian national teams in 2019. The Under-19s team winning the Australian Football Federation Youth Cup that year.

CAROL: Kai, let's discuss when you went to trial in the UK. What goals did you set yourself for your training leading up to then? What helped to keep you motivated?

KAI: I went to Burnley on trial in October 2016, and after I was offered my contract, I knew I had six months to say goodbye to home and get ready to move to the UK.

Burnley gave me a gym program to keep me ticking over, and they said while you're doing this, you're going to add a few kilos. I was 15 at the time, six feet, one inch, and proper skinny! I only weighed 60 kilos (132 pounds).

During those six months when I came back to Australia, I was really focused on the gym program they had given me and worked out sometimes 2–3 times a day. I trained so hard that I returned to the UK weighing around 75 kilos (165 pounds).

I remember when I got back over there and walked into the building, they looked at me and were like, "Far out, you've put on some muscle!" They were proper impressed, and I was really happy knowing that they could see I'd done the work.

And that's what you need in the UK. It's a physical game of football compared to Australia. I'd been given a guaranteed two-year contract at Burnley and a once-in-a-lifetime opportunity! So I knew I had to be as fit and sharp as possible. That sort of thing kept me going. If you tell me what to do, I'm going to do it. You know me—I'm a very determined guy.

CAROL: How different was the level of competition in England compared to playing in Australia? When you first started at Burnley, how did you adjust mentally to the change in intensity level?

KAI: Well, I think it's pretty obvious that football in the UK and Europe is a lot better than back home. Obviously, I hope one day Australia can get to that level, but, you know, football in Europe and England is just of a higher quality. So I knew before I came here that it was going to be physical, fast, strong ... everything about it was going to be much better. So, I already had that in my head and was mentally prepared for it.

When I went to my first trial, straight away, I was like, "Alright, these guys aren't messing around!" They could use their left foot, right foot; they were quick, they were fast ... I had to get it in my head that everything from on the pitch to off the pitch is just so strict and set.

Some other leagues are a bit more soft, but no, not over here. They don't care. They will step on your toes and elbow you. That's just how it is, and you have to deal with it. But once you get into the flow and have 10, 20, 30 games under your belt, you adapt and get used to it. Like anything, it becomes about repetition.

CAROL: Can you describe a time when you had to rely on your mental resilience during a game and what the outcome was?

KAI: Yeah, I remember two games, actually. There was one game against Blackpool in the FA Youth Cup when I was playing for Burnley, and Blackpool had a free kick on the edge of the box.

And I'm in my goal; I'd set my wall up, and I remember thinking, he's going to go right here. Well, I've stepped to the right, and he's gone back to my other side. It went in, and I knew straight away that it was my fault.

But in your head, as soon as it goes in the back of the net, you've just got to clear it out of your mind; it's gone ... get on with the rest of the game. Some people drop their heads when they concede a goal. No, as soon as you concede, set up, chest out, and head up—let's go again! ... Sorry, I made a mistake, but we'll talk about that after the game.

Photo Credit: Pedro Garcia

In another game, we had Oxford in the FA Youth Cup at Turf Moor. It was nil-nil the whole game, but I had made about five saves during the match and had made a penalty save ... but it remained nil-nil and went to penalties. We lost, unfortunately, but during the whole game it was constant back and forth, and I was excited! ... I was playing at Turf Moor, a Premier League stadium. It was only under 18s, but I was thinking, look at what I'm doing right now; imagine this stadium filled with 20,000 people.

Photo Credit: Kai Calderbank-Park

… So, it was a bit of an overwhelming experience! Like, just unbelievable! I had to keep reminding myself to stay focused. Good or bad, though, you've just gotta keep going, keep yourself positive, always be happy, smiling, head up, chest forward, and crack on with it.

CAROL: Do you do anything in particular before the game to mentally prepare? Is there anything you do to get yourself into the zone?

KAI: When I leave my house to go to the stadium, I have my earphones and just listen to my music. Then, sometimes, when I'm arriving at the stadium, I try to visualize—I think, "Alright, I'm going to save a penalty, I'm going to save a one-on-one or a 40-yard screamer, and everyone's going to be buzzing!" I'm already trying to imagine it.

When I'm getting ready, I always put on my right boot and right glove first … it's a ritual. Because I'm right-handed, I want my right glove to be tighter than my left. Mentally, I just need to feel that it's tighter … I can't have my left side tighter than my right because it feels weird.

Then I've got my customized shin pads. The one on my left is me and my girlfriend, and on the right is me and my mates from back home—my boys I grew up with. Those little things make a difference and help me mentally prepare.

CAROL: So, routine, rituals, and visualization are what help you?

KAI: Yeah, especially when I'm putting my shin pads on. The one on my left, there's my girlfriend, and I'm doing it for her. You know, I want to make her proud. And just as importantly, on my right one, I have my mates I grew up with; these are my boys back home, so I'm doing it for them. I wanna make them proud. I wanna … I don't know; it just gets me a bit emotional. When I returned home in 2019, they said I'm so proud of you … and that's what gets you; it's what inspires you.

CAROL: From a mental toughness point of view, is there anything you struggle with? Is it nerves, anxiety, self-belief, fear of injury or failure? And how are you trying to improve that aspect?

KAI: Hmmm, honestly, I'm probably one of the most laid-back, don't care type of characters. I've had people give it to me before and after the game, during games … and personally … I find it motivating and funny.

I don't get nervous. You could put me in front of 50,000 people, and I wouldn't care; I'd be like, this is great! I don't understand how players get in front of a couple of hundred people and get proper scared. No, I'm like, why? Just do your normal job. It's what you do every single day in training. What's the difference? I think, "This is cool; let's have some fun."

Even when I had an injury at Burnley, it was my second year. I injured my ankle and was out for a whole season. Long story short, the tissue that keeps your ligaments in place snapped off, so my ligaments were sliding back and forth over my ankle. I knew something didn't feel right as soon as I did it. I ended up having to have an operation and had two metal pins put in. It was about a 12-week recovery process, but then, my first running session back, one of the pins snapped, and I felt it again.

Straightaway, I looked at the physio and said, "It's gone again."

Then, when I went back to the surgeon, he said, "To be honest with you, this is going to be very difficult." There wasn't a lot of room in my ankle to secure another pin, and he told me that if it didn't work, my football career would probably be over.

But fingers crossed, and touch wood, I've been sweet since then. I remember when I did it, I was like, alright, I know I'm out for at least six months now, but I thought, I'm going to take it as a positive.

Photo Credit: Nik Mesney

CAROL: So what did you do during that recovery time?

KAI: I did a lot more analysis work just watching football. We used to go to every single Premier League game at Burnley. So I got to watch the goalkeepers, and I used to analyze them. Then I'd come back during the week with my goalkeeper coach and do some one-on-one analysis, watching the youth and under-23s.

Knowing I had six months to a year, I used it as motivation. I thought, "I'm going to get back in the gym. I'm going to get massive again. I'm going to get shredded and put some kilos on!"

We did tests before the beginning of the year, so I knew what my weaknesses were. My left foot was not as strong as my right, so I worked on my left to get it up to standard. Then, when I came back, I felt like, "Oh, I'm a machine ... here we go!". Both sides were strong and felt the same. My left ankle was even better now. I felt fresh. I hadn't kicked the ball in about a year, but I was ready to go. I was raging to get back into it with a new season coming.

So yeah, a lot of people, they get proper down, but you gotta think to turn that negative into a positive. That's always how I've seen it.

CAROL: How important do you think mental resilience is compared to physical ability in your sport, especially being a goalkeeper?

KAI: Yeah, if you don't have mental resilience as a keeper, then I don't see a point in you playing that position—you might as well just quit.

If you make one mistake, it leads to a goal. It's what gets shown all over the news and in the papers. As a goalkeeper, you need to be mentally strong. You have to realize that you're going to make mistakes. It's all about how you recover and react. As soon as you let the goal in or make a mistake, just forget it. It's gone; get on with it. The next shot that comes, you have to think, "I'm gonna save it."

… And that save could win you the game. There are so many ups and downs in a 90-minute match that it's ridiculous.

CAROL: Let's shift to your time at Wrexham. Coming into the club, and knowing that the documentary was being filmed, how did you stay focused on your training with the cameras around you?

KAI: For the first couple of days or so, I was a bit like, "What's going on?" because I'd walk down to the change room, and there'd be this massive camera with four people looking at you.

But, to be honest, within a week, you just get used to it. You generally sometimes don't even know they're there … And you make pals with the camera crew, so it just becomes normal to see them there.

Sometimes, you've also started training before they show up, so it's not a distraction or anything because you're already in training mode.

CAROL: And having Rob and Ryan show up, what was that like? Was it more motivating for you knowing they were there, or did it get into your psyche like, "I've got to perform!" Was there added pressure when they were around?

KAI: No, honestly, if anything, it motivates you even more because of how down-to-earth and lovely they are as human beings.

Photo Credit: Kai Calderbank-Park

Rob and Ryan will literally do anything for you. I remember when I was there, they pulled us aside and said that if there were anything that we wanted to do regarding the business side of football, they would help us out.

When I was thinking about starting a YouTube and Twitch channel, which I now do, they said, "Of course, yeah, we can help you out with that."

When they were there, both on and off the pitch, you could just see that they were such lovely, passionate people. The reason I'm training and playing here is because of you. They brought me in here and basically paid my wages, but they are such lovely human beings. They want to eventually take Wrexham to the Premier League, and I wanted to be part of that journey.

I can look back and say I was in that first stage when they got promoted to League 2, which is a massive achievement for Wrexham. So to be there was unbelievable; it was quite cool.

CAROL: So, from a mental resilience point of view, is there any footballer you look up to? That you respect?

KAI: When I was younger, I was actually a striker back in the day. So it was Steven Gerrard I looked up to when I was growing up.

When I became a goalkeeper, though, my idol was Hugo Lloris, who played for the Tottenham Spurs. And a lot of people say like why? … For me personally, Lloris is about the same height as me, and he played in the Premier League for about 10 or 12 years. He's a French international, was the captain for the Spurs at the time, and has captained France. He's won a World Cup. He's been one of the top keepers of our last generation for about 10 years or so.

I feel like my game is a bit like his, too. I kick the same way as him, with the ball out of my hands. So when I learned that, I was like, yeah, we are sort of similar. He's playing in the MLS now and has had an unbelievable career.

CAROL: Do you have a favorite quote, saying, or song lyric that inspires you and helps you with your journey as a footballer?

KAI: Yeah, I always say this quote. And it's literally YOLO—" You Only Live Once." For me, it's about doing as much as you can in your life.

I always say to everyone, do whatever you want. If you want to be a footballer, be a footballer; if you want to go to the moon, go to the moon … like you can do it. You've just got to put your mind to it.

I never really intended to be a footballer when I was younger. But then, two or three years later, when I went to the Wolves, I realized, you know what, I'm going alright.

Next thing you know, I signed to Burnley and thought, "Okay, this is actually going somewhere now." At that point, I was like, "Let's do it; come on!" I'm never going to have an opportunity like this again in my life, so I've got to give it my best shot.

Wholeheartedly, that's my mindset... you only live once. If you want to achieve something, go on and do it.

To watch highlights of Kai playing in the Europa League Conference scan the QR code below.

SEVEN
COACHES, TEAMMATES & MENTAL TOUGHNESS

What's your relationship with your coach and teammates like? Can you talk openly with them, or do you find yourself holding back? Do you feel comfortable in sharing your difficulties and celebrating your victories together?

In this chapter we will delve into how to strengthen relationships with your coach and teammates. Establishing strong bonds with these key figures can help lay the foundation for your mental toughness and success as an athlete.

This chapter is also just as much for your coach as it is for you. With plenty of examples on how to develop mental toughness from a team and individual player perspective, your coach will be able to create an environment where resilience is cultivated through trust, respect and teamwork, enabling you and your teammates to handle adversity and perform consistently under pressure.

TEAM CULTURE

Every successful team has a strong team culture.

So what is it?

Your team culture answers the question, "How do we actually do things? How do we get from where we are now to where we want to be?"

Your team values will influence what your team culture looks like. If someone from outside of your team walks in on a training session and watches for a while, they should be able to see your team culture. They might come out with a list of words that include the following:

- Teamwork
- Respect
- Unity
- Commitment

This person can see these things being displayed by you, your teammates, and your coach. So, your team culture is not a nice phrase that's written on a wall; it's what you are actually doing day in and day out.

To help build a strong culture, you've got to have certain things in place. It starts with establishing your team values.

Values are the nonnegotiable qualities that your team displays. They include the commitments team members make to each other and themselves. These may involve always arriving on time, wearing the correct training uniform, and agreeing to put what's best for the team first.

Once each member is transparent and committed to the values that are your team's foundation, you are ready to implement the fun things that help make them a reality.

This can involve the use of rituals, symbols and team mottos:

- **Rituals:** Rituals can include everything from special handshakes to inside jokes and acronyms. They are a powerful way to reinforce a sense of belonging to the team and its values. These shared experiences encourage camaraderie and unity among team members. Pre-game rituals, such as group huddles or listening to a specific song can boost morale and focus. Post-game rituals like singing a team song or having dinner together can provide opportunities to celebrate successes and discuss improvements collectively. These rituals contribute to building a strong team identity, where each member feels connected and committed to the group's goals, ultimately enhancing overall team performance and resilience.
- **Symbols:** A symbol might be a visual image, icon, or object with special significance. This symbol could include your club emblem, or something hanging in, or printed on the wall of your team changerooms. As part of a team ritual, you may like to acknowledge this symbol and the meaning it has to you and your team by tapping on it before a game. Additionally, wearing team colors or gear adorned with these symbols can instill pride and a sense of belonging. These symbols act as constant reminder of the team's identity, heritage, and shared mission, helping to solidify the bond amongst team members and inspire all involved to perform at their best.
- **Team Mottos:** This is a slogan or phrase that the team adopts to motivate themselves, particularly before a game. Find that one slogan that will get everyone pumped and perfectly express your team culture. Here's an example of a team motto that was proudly shouted before every match when I worked with the Wollongong Wolves Under-15's:

I am a wolf, and I will strengthen my pack!

When creating a team motto, consider the qualities or values your team embodies. You can also draw inspiration from your club's name or the traits of your club mascot.

In the Wolves example just mentioned, our team drew inspiration from this motto as it captured the essence of teamwork and unity inherent in a wolf pack. As wolves are known for their strong social connection, cooperation, and mutual support, the motto encouraged each of our players (and coaching staff), to embrace their individual responsibility while recognizing that their contributions directly enhanced the strength and success of the entire team.

Upholding this mentality was a driving force behind the incredible success we had that season, and contributed towards the team being crowned the New South Wales top tier champions!

Your team culture is strengthened by rituals, symbols and team mottos, but it also stems from values and beliefs. Those qualities distinguish a so-so culture from one that propels a team to greatness, promoting cohesion, resilience, and a shared sense of purpose among its members.

BUILDING POSITIVE COACH-ATHLETE RELATIONSHIPS

In sports, coaches aren't just there to teach you drills or strategies; they're there to guide you through athletic ups and downs both on and off the field. Consequently, they can become your ultimate ally in building resilience. However, establishing a winning relationship with your coach doesn't just happen automatically. You and your coach have to work at creating it.

Here are some fundamental elements needed to build a positive relationship with your coach:

- **Mutual Respect:** Having a shared sense of respect for each other is essential to this relationship. When you respect your coach, and they respect you back, magic happens! You feel comfortable sharing your ideas, asking questions, and working

together. Plus, it builds trust, which is the glue that holds everything together.
- **Communication:** This is key to helping develop mutual respect. Talk to your coach honestly and kindly, just like you'd want them to talk to you. Listen to their feedback, even if it's tough to hear, and don't be afraid to share your thoughts and feelings.
- **Appreciation:** Be grateful for all the hard work your coach puts in. A simple "thank you" or high-five after practice can go a long way. It shows that you see and value their effort. This won't go unnoticed by your coach and will make them feel appreciated.
- **Teamwork:** This is another way to gain the respect of your coach. When you support your teammates and cheer them on, you also respect your coach's leadership. It's like saying, "Hey, coach, we're all in this together, and we've got your back!" This is particularly important even when your coach hasn't picked you in the starting line-up or has substituted you off. Showing that you can respect their decision and put your own disappointment aside to encourage your teammates will be something that your coach will again take notice of and value.

THREE FAMOUS SPORTS PARTNERSHIPS

There have been numerous coach-athlete partnerships over the years that have embodied what a positive and trusting relationship should look like. Here are three standouts that both you and your coach can draw inspiration from:

#1: Michael Jordan and Phil Jackson

The relationship between Michael Jordan and Phil Jackson is legendary in sports. Their partnership led to unparalleled success on the basketball court and left a lasting legacy in the world of coaching and leadership. Let's dive into what made their bond so special and how

Jackson earned Jordan's undying loyalty while bringing out the best in him.

First and foremost, trust was the cornerstone of their relationship. Phil Jackson understood Jordan's unparalleled talent and recognized the importance of empowering him as a leader. He trusted Michael's instincts on the court and allowed him to express himself as a player and leader. This mutual trust fostered a deep sense of respect, laying the foundation for their success.

Jackson's coaching philosophy was another critical factor in their relationship. He wasn't just a basketball coach but a master of psychology and team dynamics. Jackson embraced uncommon methods, such as Zen Buddhism and Native American rituals, to instill a sense of mindfulness and unity within the team. This approach connected with Jordan, who thrived under Jackson's mental and emotional guidance.

Jackson also understood the importance of managing egos and building a solid team culture. He created an environment where every player felt valued and understood their role within the team. Instead of relying solely on Jordan's brilliance, Jackson emphasized teamwork and collective effort. This approach elevated Jordan's game and empowered his teammates to contribute to the team's success.

Another crucial aspect of their relationship was Jackson's ability to challenge Jordan. He wasn't afraid to push Michael out of his comfort zone and demand more from him, both on and off the court. Jackson knew how to balance support and tough love, motivating Jordan to strive for excellence continuously. Michael respected Jackson's coaching philosophy and embraced his role as a mentor, recognizing the value of Jackson's guidance in his journey toward greatness.

Ultimately, their relationship was special because of their mutual respect, trust, and understanding. Their partnership resulted in six NBA championships and transformed how we view coaching and leadership in sports.

#2: Serena Williams and Partick Mouratoglou

The relationship between Serena Williams and Patrick Mouratoglou is a fascinating tale of collaboration and respect. At the heart of their bond was a deep mutual trust. Mouratoglou, a renowned tennis coach, understood Serena's immense talent and shared her relentless drive for success. He believed in her abilities and provided unwavering support, creating a safe space for Serena to thrive on and off the court.

Mouratoglou's coaching approach went beyond technical skills, focusing on mental toughness, tactical strategies, and physical fitness. He tailored his coaching to suit Serena's unique strengths and weaknesses, constantly pushing her to evolve and adapt her game. By challenging her to step out of her comfort zone and embrace new tactics, Mouratoglou helped Serena take her game to unprecedented levels.

One of Mouratoglou's greatest strengths as a coach was providing constructive feedback while maintaining a positive and supportive atmosphere. He understood the importance of nurturing Serena's confidence and self-belief, encouraging her to build upon her strengths and play with conviction.

Mouratoglou built a culture of accountability and continuous improvement within their team. He encouraged open communication and collaboration, inviting Serena to actively participate in the decision-making process and take ownership of her development. In this way Mouratoglou helped empower Serena to unleash her full potential on the court.

#3: Christiano Ronaldo and Sir Alex Ferguson

The relationship between Cristiano Ronaldo and Sir Alex Ferguson is one of the most iconic in football history. Their partnership brought unprecedented success to Manchester United and transformed Ronaldo into one of the greatest players of all time.

Sir Alex saw Ronaldo's potential when he signed him for Manchester United as a young talent from Sporting Lisbon. He believed in

Ronaldo's abilities and provided the guidance and support he needed to flourish on the pitch. The trust that was built between them created a strong foundation for their relationship and allowed Ronaldo to thrive under Sir Alex's mentorship.

Sir Alex recognized Ronaldo's raw talent and instilled in him the discipline, work ethic, and tactical smarts required to succeed at the highest level. He challenged Ronaldo to push beyond his limits and constantly strive for improvement.

Sir Alex understood the importance of building up Ronaldo's confidence and self-belief. He encouraged Ronaldo to express himself on the pitch and play with the freedom and creativity that has defined his style of play. Sir Alex provided constructive feedback and guidance, but also allowed Ronaldo the chance to make his own decisions and take risks.

Another critical aspect of their relationship was Sir Alex's ability to create a supportive and competitive environment within the team. He developed a culture of unity and accountability, where players were encouraged to push each other to be their best. This environment motivated Ronaldo to continuously raise his game and strive for excellence, knowing his teammates and manager had his back.

Finally, Sir Alex showed genuine care and interest in Ronaldo's well-being both on and off the pitch. For Cristiano this created a sense of loyalty, family, and respect that has stood the test of time and remains strong between the two of them to this day.

LEARNING FROM THE GREATS

Now that we've explored three great examples of what coach-athlete partnerships can look like, let's examine some key elements. Take the time to read over these relationships again and see if you can list any common trends in the way Phil, Patrick, and Sir Alex worked with their respective athlete. Write them down here:

Coaching Element #1:

_____
_____
_____

Coaching Element #2:

_____
_____
_____

Coaching Element #3:

_____
_____
_____

Now, consider the relationship you have with your coach. Rate the elements you've identified on a scale between 1 to 10 based on how effectively they are shown in your own coach-athlete relationship.

Finally, think about how you can improve these ratings with your coach. Take the time to also factor in those elements described previously that help to build a positive coach-athlete relationship such as mutual respect, communication, appreciation, and teamwork.

COACHES CORNER: BUILDING POSITIVE COACH-ATHLETE RELATIONSHIPS

As a coach, you have a unique opportunity to shape your young athletes' skills and fortify their minds not only for sports, but the game of life. Let's explore some strategies for cultivating mental toughness and strengthening the bond between you, your team, and individual athletes.

Lead by Example: We can't expect our athletes to develop mental toughness if we don't embody it ourselves. Share your experiences of overcoming challenges and staying resilient. For example, if you have previously played sports, share a story about your time as an athlete or a challenging situation you have faced as a coach. Showing vulnerability helps humanize you in the eyes of your team and inspires them to push through their own difficulties.

Be Empathetic: Showing empathy goes a long way in helping a young athlete navigate not only the ups and downs of competitive sports, but life in general. Be mindful of and respect that sometimes other life events take priority over their sporting commitments. These can include a family wedding, or sadly, even funerals. Alternatively, your young athlete may also require a night or two off training to study for an important school exam. Be understanding and accommodate these needs when they arise, always providing a supportive environment where they are not penalized for these events taking priority.

Mentoring Moments: Take time to talk to your athletes individually at training and on game days. These mentoring moments could be as simple as providing feedback during rest breaks between training drills, or something more formal to discuss their individual goals, or performances strengths and weaknesses (including parents or caregivers in these structured conversations can also be beneficial.) You'll build rapport with your athletes by showing a genuine interest in their individual development.

Active Involvement: Instead of being the only one leading conversations and dictating the direction of training sessions, allow your young athletes to have a more proactive role in their development. By encouraging open discussion, actively listening to feedback, and allowing your athletes to try new things (even if they don't work out!), you will help to foster a greater sense of ownership and accountability amongst your players. This can help make them feel more invested in their training and provide you both with some invaluable learning and teachable moments.

Engaging in such practices helps young athletes develop their decision making and problem-solving skills. It allows them to analyze their strengths and weaknesses, and collaboratively explore solutions. This can significantly enhance their mental resilience as they learn to navigate challenges and setbacks with a more proactive and independent mindset. It will additionally build their confidence and communication skills, preparing them to make informed decisions during the heat of competition.

THE IMPORTANCE OF MENTORSHIP IN ATHLETE DEVELOPMENT

Imagine walking up a mountain trail you've never been on before. You get to a fork in the road and decide to go left. After an hour, you realize you're slowly heading downhill—you've chosen the wrong direction! Now, you've got to retrace your steps to get back to the level you were at previously.

How much better would it have been if you'd had a guide alongside you—someone who could warn you about all the tracks that can lead you in the wrong direction?

A mentor can be that guide for you.

As seen with Tom Brady's story in Chapter One, a mentor doesn't necessarily have to be your coach. One of the most influential people in Tom's playing career was his university sports psychologist.

Examples of other individuals who can help mentor you through your athletic journey include:

- **Retired Athletes:** A retired athlete's career can serve as a roadmap to success. They've undoubtedly stumbled, had moments of misjudgment, and perhaps followed the wrong advice. By learning from their journey, you can steer clear of the same mistakes and make informed decisions.
- **Senior Teammates/Players in Older Age Groups:** Similar to the above, these more seasoned athletes can also provide you with invaluable knowledge based on their past experiences. However, the added bonus with these mentors is that you get to witness how they handle the ups and downs of competition in real-time. If you are fortunate enough to be playing in the same team as these mentors, they are often also great at providing on-the-go pieces of advice to learn from.
- **Assistant Coaching Staff:** These people could include a team manager, assistant coach, conditioning coach, or a health professional such as a physiotherapist. Depending on their position within the team and area of expertise, these people can help build your resilience in different ways. For example, a conditioning coach can guide you through the do's and don'ts of what it takes to excel physically at your sport. At the same time, a physiotherapist may be able to provide you with the psychological reassurance and education you need while recovering from an injury.
- **School Teachers:** As a student athlete, school teachers can be invaluable in helping you find a balance between your athletic endeavors and schoolwork. They can assist you in prioritizing your time and find ways to help you manage potential academic stressors such as poor study routines or low grades.

Keep an eye out for these incredible people and how their wisdom and experience can help shape your mindset as an athlete—and person, now and for many years to come!

YOU AND YOUR TEAMMATES

Being part of a team is one of the most incredible benefits of playing sports. It can give you a deep sense of belonging, pride, and support. A strong team environment also helps you build resilience when things get tough. Knowing your teammates have your back can help you bounce back from setbacks and challenges.

But it's not all plain sailing.

In any group, you'll have people with whom you get along better than others, and maybe one or two with whom you just don't gel. Your challenge is to keep that from affecting your team's cohesion.

Here are some tips to help you play your part in creating a solid team bond:

- **Focus on the Common Goal:** It's not about making a bunch of new friends (though that would be nice!) but about improving and being as successful as possible. You might not get along socially with every team member, but don't lose sight of what the team is about—performing well together.
- **Appreciate Everyone's Role:** Focus on what each player brings to the team and how you all work collaboratively to create the best performance outcome. Even if you don't naturally get along with a player, they are still a valuable part of the team as are you. Everyone has a role to play in achieving success, and acknowledging this can help build unity and respect.
- **Lead By Example:** Demonstrate a positive attitude, work ethic, and sportsmanship both on and off the field. Show commitment and respect toward your teammates and coach by striving to be punctual, prepared, and focused during training and on game day, always aiming to maintain a supportive and encouraging demeanor. By consistently displaying these qualities, you inspire others to follow suit,

creating a culture of excellence and mutual respect within the team.

COACH'S CORNER: TEAM COHESION

Even the most cohesive team will have bumpy periods where conflict arises. As a youth sports coach, you work with young people who are still developing the social skills needed to create team cohesion. Here are some ideas to help you build a cohesive team environment:

- **Establish Team Values & Goals:** During preseason, hold a theory-based session to establish team values and goals for the upcoming season. This works well when it is player-led. Divide the team into small groups to discuss and write down what their desired goals and values are. Each team must then present their ideas to the rest of the squad. This activity encourages open communication, teamwork, and the chance for everyone to contribute towards what the team wants to achieve for the season and the values that will help get them there. This activity allows for a sense of ownership and responsibility toward maintaining the standards they themselves have established and agreed upon. (This session is also a great opportunity for brainstorming team mottos!).
- **Provide Fun Warm-Up Activities:** At training, provide fun and engaging small group warm-ups that are competitive but foster camaraderie and friendship among teammates. These warm-up exercises don't necessarily have to be related to your particular sport either. So long as players are appropriately warmed up get creative and allow your team to have some fun!
- **Create Team Rituals:** As mentioned earlier in this chapter, this could be as simple as shaking each other's hands at the start and end of training, gathering in a huddle and chanting a team motto before games, or singing a team song after a

competitive win. These team rituals encourage respect, a sense of belonging, and team unity.
- **Organize a Team-Bonding Event:** Allowing your team to get to know one another away from the training pitch can be a great way to build team cohesion. Organizing events such as team dinners or fun activities like ten-pin bowling or putt-putt golf can be a lighthearted way for your players to strengthen their team bond.

Conflict Resolution

Hopefully, this will not happen often. However, should an incident occur and your involvement is required, here's an eight-step guide on how you can help manage conflicts when they arise between your athletes:

1. **Identify the issue:** Begin by identifying the conflict or issue at hand. Listen to everyone involved and gather information about the situation.
2. **Establish ground rules:** Set boundaries for the conflict resolution process, emphasizing the importance of respectful communication and active listening. Ensure that everyone can express their thoughts and feelings without interruption.
3. **Encourage open communication:** Promote a safe and supportive environment that lets your young athletes feel comfortable raising their concerns. Encourage open dialogue and ensure that every voice is heard.
4. **Focus on solutions:** Move the focus from blaming or criticizing to finding constructive solutions. Brainstorm potential resolutions together while emphasizing that some give-and-take is needed to help resolve the issue.
5. **Seek common ground:** Identify areas of agreement and common interests among the players involved. Use these as a foundation for finding mutually acceptable solutions.

6. **Develop an action plan:** Once a resolution has been reached, develop a clear action plan outlining the steps that need to be taken to address the conflict and prevent it from recurring in the future. Assign responsibilities and set deadlines as required.
7. **Follow up:** Follow up with the players involved to ensure the resolution is implemented effectively and address any lingering concerns or issues. Continue to monitor the situation and provide assistance as needed to prevent further conflicts from arising.
8. **Ongoing support:** Offer continued support and guidance to the athletes involved in the conflict resolution process. Emphasize the importance of learning from conflicts and using them as opportunities for personal and team growth.

NAVIGATING COMPETITIVE FRIENDSHIPS: HEALTHY RIVALRIES

Sometimes friendships can get pretty competitive. This can be exciting yet tricky. It's like walking a tightrope between being buddies and rivals while trying to have fun and do well in your sport.

Let's take some time to consider the pros and cons of competitive rivalries and then explore some tactics to navigate them.

The Good Stuff

- **Motivation Boost:** When you are surrounded by friends or teammates that are both competitive and supportive it can be super motivating. When you see them doing well, it can push you to try harder and be your best too. This positive environment creates a healthy amount of competition that fuels your desire to improve both individually and as a team.
- **Getting Better Together:** Competitive friendships can help you both improve your technical and tactical abilities by practicing together. One-on-one training allows you to practice specific moves you may want to work on with

focused attention. This often provides you with a greater amount of repetition than what team training sessions are likely to allow. By offering constructive feedback and learning from one another's strengths and weaknesses, you'll both improve your athletic ability and performance.
- **Shared Experiences:** It is probable within a competitive sporting friendship that you and your friend have experienced some similar high and lows that come with being an athlete. Discussing challenges and concerns with your friend can help reduce stress and provide an outlet for venting frustrations, seeking advice, and receiving encouragement.

The Tricky Parts

- **Feeling Left Out:** Sometimes, seeing your friend or teammates succeed can make you feel a bit jealous or left out, especially if you're having a tough time with your own performance. When this occurs try your best to put these emotions aside when around them and just be happy to share in their success.
- **Comparing Yourself:** It's common to compare yourself to your friend and feel like you're not good enough. But you must try to remember that everyone has their strengths and it's okay to be different. Everybody's journey is unique and comparing yourself to others can be detrimental to your self-esteem and progress. Instead of focusing on how you measure up to your friend, concentrate on your personal growth and achievements, recognizing that everyone progresses at their own pace.
- **Friendship Struggles:** When competition gets too intense, it can strain your friendship. Arguments and misunderstandings might pop up, and that's no fun for anyone. Remember that your friendship should be a source of strength and support, not stress and conflict. Finding a balance between being competitive and being supportive can help ensure that your

friendship remains strong, even in the face of intense competition.

Tips for Navigating Competitive Friendships

- **Keep it Cool:** Do your best to prioritize your relationship and recognize that sports and competition are just one aspect of your lives and should play a small role in your overall friendship. Don't let it take over. Focus on having fun and supporting each other.
- **Talk it Out:** If things start feeling weird between you and your friend, talk about it. Be honest and respectful, and listen to what they have to say too. Let your friend know how much their friendship means to you and that you value their perspective. Conversations like this can help clear the air, reinforcing your bond and preventing minor issues from escalating into bigger problems.
- **Set Some Rules:** Agree on some ground rules with your friend to keep things fair and friendly, especially when you are training or competing against one another. For example, no trash-talking or comparing achievements.
- **Be Your Own Hero:** Instead of trying to outshine your friend, focus on being the best version of yourself. Set personal goals, and work diligently toward them—regardless of what your friend is doing.

RAFA AND ROGER: THE ULTIMATE COMPETITIVE FRIENDSHIP ROLE MODELS

Rafael Nadal and Roger Federer are the ultimate example of what a competitive friendship should be! They share such a strong bond that the name "Fedal" has been coined when the two are spoken about together.

They have competed against each other in many high-stakes matches, including multiple Grand Slam finals, where the competition is intense and the pressure is high. However, their competitive rivalry has always stayed on the court and never affected their friendship.

Nadal and Federer have spoken openly about admiring each other's skills and accomplishments. They have often praised each other's playing style, work ethic, and sportsmanship. Despite their competitive nature, they have always supported and encouraged one another in victories and defeats.

Over the years, they have enjoyed socializing at various tennis events, charity functions and have done multiple interviews together, often laughing with each other and showcasing their friendship.

One of the most iconic moments they shared was in 2022, when they played together in the Laver Cup. Roger had announced that the tournament would be his last before retiring. There was not a dry eye in the house as the duo embraced each other multiple times, both visibly upset that this would be the last time they would compete together.

Nadal and Federer have shown that fierce competition and genuine friendship can coexist. Their relationship illustrates the true spirit of sportsmanship and serves as an inspiring example for young athletes everywhere. Together, they have proven that rivalry can drive excellence while still respecting and valuing each other as friends.

CHAPTER SEVEN: THREE KEY POINTS I NEED TO WORK ON

I Need To:

1. _____
2. _____
3. _____

How I'll Do It:

1. _____
2. _____
3. _____

When I'll Check My Progress:

1. _____
2. _____
3. _____

EIGHT
INVOLVING FAMILY

How did you get into your sport? Who provided the opportunities, encouraged you when you were unsure, and paid for your uniform and training gear? Who drove you to and from practice, rain, hail or shine, without hesitation or complaint?

Most likely, the answer is your parents. They're the ones who provided the support base so you could get established in this passion for sports that you've come to embrace. Now that you're older, the importance of your family doesn't lessen. It's just as crucial now as it has always been.

As you've matured, your relationship with your parents has naturally transformed. Perhaps, in the past, you felt a surge of pride when your mom cheered you on from the sidelines, but now you find the thought of it a bit embarrassing. As you're stepping into your identity, it's natural to desire some independence.

However, your relationship with your parents is still a cornerstone of your athletic success. When strong and loving relationships are cultivated with your family, it lays a foundation of safety, security, and belonging. As a young person and athlete, when you feel loved and valued as an individual you are less vulnerable to other people's harsh criticisms or actions. Your identity serves as an anchor, so the negativity of others simply washes over you.

In this chapter, we'll explore how the people closest to you—your family—play a crucial role in shaping your journey as an athlete. We'll also explore what you and your family members can do to ensure that the support you're getting is constructive rather than restrictive, empowering rather than limiting, and nurturing rather than stifling.

I encourage you to read this chapter with your parents. Then, talk about how you can continue to work together in your development as an athlete and a person.

COMMUNICATING WITH YOUR PARENTS

As you grow older, your communication with parents can undergo significant changes. It can become more complex, and involve deeper discussions about personal values, future goals, and social issues. While this can sometimes lead to misunderstandings and conflicts, it also provides an opportunity for you and your parents to build a stronger, more mature relationship based on mutual respect and open, honest discussions.

Here are two ways you can help improve your communication with your parents:

Talk About Feelings

Understanding your feelings is a big part of staying in control of your emotions and not becoming overwhelmed. So, rather than pulling away from your parents, work hard to strengthen your communication with them.

Sometimes, the words you say and the message that your parent gets is quite different. Let's say your mom notices you're in a bad mood after training and she asks what's wrong. You reply that you don't want to talk about it, and then start texting on your phone. But the message your mom receives is that you don't trust her enough to confide in her and would rather open up to your friends.

When talking to your parents about your performance, it's easy to think, "What would they know," or "You just don't get it," especially if they haven't played sports. Even if this is the case, please do not discount the value of their other life experiences and the simple fact that they know and love you. This alone is incredibly valuable because their perspective can provide wisdom and guidance that might not immediately be apparent. Their support can offer comfort and reassurance, helping you navigate the physical and emotional challenges of being an athlete. So, don't hesitate to share your feelings with them; their care and insight can be instrumental in your athletic journey.

Listen

Listening to your parents doesn't mean thoughtlessly following their advice or agreeing with everything they say. It's about being respectful, open-minded, and willing to learn.

When your parents are talking to you, put down your phone or any other distractions and give them your full attention. Make eye contact and actively listen to show them you value what they have to say.

Even if you don't always agree with your mom or dad's perspective, try to keep an open mind. Remember that they have your best interests at heart and may offer valuable insights or advice based on their own experiences.

Feel free to ask questions if you need clarification. This shows you're engaged in the conversation and eager to learn from their wisdom.

Let your parents know you appreciate their support and guidance. A simple "thank you" can go a long way in strengthening your relationship and encouraging them to continue offering their help.

When your parents offer feedback or constructive criticism, take some time to reflect on it. Instead of getting defensive, consider their perspective and how you can use their input to improve as an athlete and a person.

PARENT'S CORNER: COMMUNICATION AND SUPPORT

Sometimes, minimizing your child's negative experience can be tempting, such as saying something like, "It wasn't that bad," or, "It's over now, so let's just forget about it." But when you stop your child from feeling or owning their emotions, you prevent them from understanding and learning how to deal with them.

So, please, encourage them to talk through their feelings rather than distracting or blocking them out. Listen empathetically and validate their feelings with statements like, "That sounds really hard" or, "I can see how disappointed you are." This kind of active listening shows your child that their feelings are valid and important. Work with them to brainstorm ideas and actively seek solutions to the issues they are facing together. This approach not only strengthens your bond but also empowers your child to develop emotional resilience and problem-solving skills, essential for their overall well-being and success in both sports and life.

Balancing Encouragement and Pressure

Finding the balance between encouragement and pressure as an athlete parent can be challenging. Encouragement offers positive reinforcement and support. It's motivating and feeds the child's self-efficacy. Pressure has the opposite effect. It's when you push too hard, overemphasize winning, and don't give your child room to breathe. It leads children on a path to anxiety, unhappiness, and burnout.

A key difference is that encouragement is built on effort and improvement, while pressure is usually outcome based.

An encouraging statement might be, "Just go out there and give it your best shot. Win or lose, I'm here to support you."

In contrast, a pressure-inducing statement could be, "I know you can do it; we really need this win today. Make sure you play your absolute best and bring home the victory."

Encouraging feedback is constructive, setting up growth opportunities, while pressure feedback tends to be negative, with acceptance conditioned upon performance. It's your responsibility to use your voice and actions to ease rather than add to the difficulties of being a student-athlete and provide the encouraging support system your child needs.

Here are some ways you can find the right balance between encouragement and pressure:

- Emphasize the importance of enjoying the sport.
- Never compare your child to anyone else.
- Help your child live a balanced life, including studying, socializing, and resting.
- Encourage your child to be a self-motivator who sets goals and has high personal standards.
- Exemplify good sportsmanship, especially when watching them compete.
- Celebrate their effort rather than success alone.
- Respect your child's boundaries; do not become overbearing or controlling.
- Be an advocate for your child's coach; don't criticize their decisions in front of your child.

The Supportive Home Environment

Young athletes must have a safe and supportive home base. This is where they can recharge physically and emotionally after intense training sessions and competitions. In their home environment, athletes should feel free to express themselves, share their triumphs and challenges, and receive unwavering support from their family members.

Below are ways in which families can be involved in an athlete's training and competition in a supportive and positive manner:

- **Show Up:** Families can create a supportive environment by being present during competitions and celebrating the athlete's achievements, regardless of the competitive outcome. Being present at games, matches, or tournaments sends a powerful message of encouragement and belief in their abilities. This helps build the athlete's confidence and motivation, knowing that their family is behind them every step of the way. Taking the time to also engage in meaningful discussions after the performance shows a young athlete that their family's involvement goes beyond mere attendance and extends into a deeper level of engagement with their sporting endeavors.
- **Offer Logistical Support:** Families can assist with the practical aspects of training and competition, such as transportation to and from practices, organizing equipment, and coordinating schedules. This support can reduce stress for both the athlete and the family as a whole.
- **Support Nutritional Goals:** Proper nutrition is crucial for athletic performance and recovery. Family members can ensure that their young athlete has access to nutritious meals and snacks that support their training and competition regimen. This also includes discouraging and/or limiting unhealthy fast food options after training or match play.
- **Volunteer:** As parents, volunteering your time to help not only your young athlete, but also the club they play for demonstrates how invested you are in their journey. Volunteer roles could include anything from being a team manager to help ensure all administrative tasks and game day requirements are met, to offering a hand in running the club canteen.
- **Help Assess Performances and Techniques:** Parents can play a significant role in evaluating your young athlete's performances and techniques. This might involve observing

their training sessions and providing immediate feedback or sitting down together to analyze an entire performance. For the latter, it is beneficial to let your child take the lead in this analysis. Encourage them to identify both the strengths and areas for improvement in their performance. To facilitate this, ask thought-provoking questions like, "What do you notice about your body positioning?" or "What do you think you could do better next time?" This approach promotes self-assessment and problem-solving, allowing them to develop a deeper awareness of the technical and tactical aspects of their performance before you offer additional feedback.
- **Encourage Balance:** Young athletes must balance sports and other aspects of their lives, such as academics and social activities. Families can help by encouraging their young athlete to prioritize their school work appropriately through regularly scheduling time to study around training and competition. Additionally encouraging quality time spent with friends, or performing hobbies unrelated to sport, can be great ways to for an athlete to destress and recharge both physically and mentally away from the rigours of their athletic schedule.
- **Communicate with Coaches:** Open communication between families and coaches is essential for a young athlete's development. As a parent, look to build positive relationships with coaches, exchanging feedback and discussing your child's progress and goals.

SIBLINGS

Growing up with siblings is like having built-in best friends who stick with you for life. The bond you share with them is unique, filled with shared memories, inside jokes, and a deep understanding of each other that only comes from growing up together.

When it comes to your journey as a youth athlete, siblings can be your biggest cheerleaders, toughest competitors, and most reliable supporters. Their constant presence make the ups and downs of sports more enjoyable and meaningful, helping you become the best athlete—and person you can be.

Here are some of the fantastic ways your siblings can help build your resilience as an athlete:

- **Skill Development:** Having siblings at home provides frequent opportunities to practice your skills outside of team training sessions, whether after school, on weekends, or during the off-season. They can offer valuable feedback and observations on your performance, adding another perspective to your development as an athlete. There is also ample opportunity for enthusiastic and detailed discussions about your performances, enabling you to try new things or fine-tune specific skills.
- **Push Limits:** When there is a healthy amount of sibling rivalry, the physicality of training with a sibling can help build the same sort of physical and mental resilience needed during competition. More than your friends and teammates, siblings have a unique ability to push your limits. Often you may find yourself being "polite" when it comes to training with friends or teammates, and perhaps hold back a little because these people are your friends. However when training with a sibling you can test boundaries. Politeness goes out the window and it's game on! This dynamic can allow you to develop the competitive edge necessary for success in your sport.
- **Mentors:** If you have an older sibling who is also involved in sport they can serve as an excellent role model, demonstrating hard work, dedication, and good sportsmanship. Experienced siblings can also provide advice on how to handle coaches, training routines, and balancing sports with other responsibilities.
- **Emotional Support:** When a close bond is shared between you and your sibling, it can often be that they will be one of,

(if not the first) person you go to for emotional support. Siblings also have a knack for delivering criticisms in way that can soften the blow due to the compassionate and trusted nature of the relationship. When you have someone close to you who you feel safe opening up to and whose feedback is delivered in a way that is easy to absorb, it helps build mental toughness. This supportive relationship allows you to face challenges and setbacks with greater resilience, knowing you have a reliable and constant source of encouragement and constructive advice.

BALANCING SPORTS AND SOCIAL LIFE: A FAMILY AFFAIR

It can be challenging to balance your sports commitments with having an actual life, like going to the movies and out for dinner. To make it work, you'll need the support and involvement of your family.

As with every part of a successful family, it starts with good communication. Share your schedule, commitments, and social plans with your family. Sit down together and determine what needs to be prioritized and how you can make it all work.

Sports schedules can sometimes get crazy, especially during big events or busy seasons. Work with your parents to set clear boundaries around your sports and social activities to ensure you're not overdoing it in either area. Prioritize schoolwork and self-care while still making time for the things you enjoy.

Even with your busy schedule, work hard to make time for family activities and bonding. Whether it's a weekend hike, a movie night, or just hanging out at home, those moments together are golden and will become memories you'll cherish for years to come. Never underestimate the value of this time spent together and how much it will also mean to your parents and siblings as you grow older.

Serena Williams is an excellent example of an athlete who has corrected the imbalance in her sporting and social life. Serena has faced challenges on and off the court. Throughout her career, she has experienced periods of burnout and struggled with balancing the demands of professional tennis with her personal life. Despite facing criticism and setbacks, Williams has learned over time to prioritize self-care and balance her career, family, and interests outside of tennis.

Another famous athlete who knows the value of family is David Beckham. In the early stages of their relationship, the English football superstar always found the time to step away from his hectic training schedule to spend time with his girlfriend, and now wife, Victoria. Since becoming a parent David has also prioritized time with his family. In an interview that focused on his life as parent, Beckham emphasised the importance of "being present" when he spends time with his family. He stated that hiking, as well as playing games, and simply being together away from any other distractions is what he cherishes the most.

By creating a harmonious balance between your sporting ambitions, school work, and quality time with family and friends, you'll cultivate a well-rounded environment and lifestyle. This approach will help to keep you grounded, focused, and not only lead to sustained athletic success, but also nurture your overall happiness.

Remember, true success is not just about excelling in sports; it's about finding joy, fulfillment, and contentment in every part of your life, and sharing these moments with those who love and support you the most.

CHAPTER EIGHT: THREE KEY POINTS I NEED TO WORK ON

I Need To:

1. _____

2. _____

3. _____

How I'll Do It:

1. _____

2. _____

3. _____

When I'll Check My Progress:

1. _____

2. _____

3. _____

FULL TIME

This book hasn't done a thing to directly improve your physical skills. It hasn't taught you how to dunk, tackle, or score goals. Instead, we've focused on something far more powerful—the qualities that lie beneath the surface.

It's like an iceberg. The part you see are the skills that you display during competition. But it's what lies underneath that truly defines your success.

So what are these qualities?

It's what we've explored in every chapter of this journey:

A Growth Mindset: Embracing adversity, learning from mistakes, and believing in your ability to improve—it's what champions are made of. With a growth mindset, you're not just a player but a constantly evolving athlete, ready to conquer any challenge.

Resilience: Think back to resilience—the power to bounce back from challenges and emerge even stronger. It's not just about your skills; it's about the inner strength that defines a true athlete and champion.

Perseverance: Perseverance is the determination to keep pushing forward when the going gets tough. Your skills are a testament to your hard work, but it's your perseverance that will carry you on toward greatness.

Positivity: A positive outlook turns challenges into opportunities. Your skills shine brightest when fueled by positivity and self-belief.

Staying Focused: Distractions can be hurdles, but staying focused sharpens your skills. Your ability to focus elevates your performance on and off the field.

Overcoming Adversity: Life, like sports, throws curveballs. We've explored how overcoming obstacles builds character and strength. Your skills aren't just for wins but for rising stronger after every fall.

Goal Setting: Setting clear goals gives your athletic journey direction. Your ability to set and pursue goals is what turns potential into achievement.

Self-Belief: Your skills are impressive, but it's the unshakeable belief in yourself that propels you forward. You've always had the potential; now you have the mindset to match.

These skills have laid the foundation for your athletic excellence. Continue working on them as you would a muscle, and they will give you the mental toughness you need to excel in competition.

But they'll do more than that.

The mental toughness skills we've explored in this book will ensure that life's curveballs won't knock you down; they'll only make you stronger. Remember that a growth mindset is not just for sports—it's a mindset for life, where challenges become exciting growth opportunities. It's a mindset that can guide you in any endeavor you choose to pursue.

So, as you continue to hone these mental skills, remember they are also tools for becoming the resilient, focused, and confident individual you aspire to be both on and off the field.

However, even with all of the mental toughness skills we've been developing, you can't do it all yourself.

You are not an island.

Remember the importance of a supportive environment. Your coaches, mentors, family, teammates, and friends are your cheerleaders and guides. They play a crucial role in shaping and sustaining your mental resilience. When you have a nurturing support system around you, challenges become easier to tackle, and your goals become more achievable. So don't hesitate to lean on them, learn from them, and let their support propel you to new heights. Together with your mental toughness and their unwavering guidance, there's no limit to what you can accomplish.

…Now, before we part ways, I want to get real with you.

In this book, you have learned about the most powerful mental toughness skills for athletes. But just learning about them will not help you to improve.

It's now up to you to **apply** them.

You see, the vast majority of people who buy self-improvement books like this one will often read through them enthusiastically, agree that they should put the advice into practice, and then do … absolutely nothing!

But not you, right?

I know you're different. You're a young athlete with a hunger for growth and self development.

So here's the challenge: take what you've learned and make it a part of your daily life. When you step onto the field, bring your positive mindset, perseverance, and focus. When challenges arise, face them head-on with resilience and determination.

And don't forget about the power of self-reflection. It's like looking in the mirror at your mind. Take time to think about your experiences, your successes, and even your setbacks. What can you learn from them and how can you improve?

Consistency is key. Just like you train your body regularly, train your mind too. Practice these mental toughness exercises like they're part of your warm-up routine. They'll become second nature, making you not just a better athlete but a better person.

With dedication, practice, and a positive mindset, you can overcome any challenge and realize your full potential.

The journey to greatness starts now.

Go out there, dream big, work hard, and become the absolute champion you were born to be!

Success is in the effort. —J. Cole

AFTER THE GAME

My aim for this book is to make becoming a resilient young athlete accessible to all. Everything I do stems from that mission. And, the only way for me to accomplish it is by reaching…well…everyone!

Now that you have everything you need to become a resilient young athlete (or a more informed parent or coach), it's time to pass on your newfound knowledge and show other readers where they can find the same help.

By leaving your honest opinion of this book on Amazon, you'll be guiding other youth athletes to the tools and tips they need to thrive. Your review can inspire others to discover the same strategies, motivation, and mental toughness that you've gained from these pages.

The spirit of resilience is kept alive when we share our experiences and insights. Help me to spread this valuable knowledge and words of encouragement to those who need it most.

You review could help…

…one more young athlete find their inner strength.

…one more player bounce back from a tough game.

...one more teammate stay motivated.

...one more kid realize their dreams.

Please scan the relevant QR code below, or navigate to the Amazon marketplace where you purchased this copy to leave a review.

Amazon.com

Amazon.com.au

Thank you for your support,

Carol Robins.

BIBLIOGRAPHY

Australian Open TV (Director). (2022, January 30). *Rafael Nadal v Daniil Medvedev full match (Final) | Australian Open 2022*. https://www.youtube.com/watch?v=6I06-ITW88k

Blackwell, L. S., Trzesniewski, K. H., & Dweck, C. S. (2007). Implicit theories of intelligence predict achievement across an adolescent transition: A longitudinal study and an intervention. *Child Development, 78*(1), 246–263. https://doi.org/10.1111/j.1467-8624.2007.00995.x

Chengelis, A. S. (2020, June 29). *For 34 years, Greg Harden has been Michigan student-athletes' 'miracle worker'*. Retrieved June 13, 2024, from https://www.detroitnews.com/story/sports/college/university-michigan/2020/06/30/greg-harden-has-been-michigan-student-athletes-miracle-worker/3278576001/

Cox, D., Dr (2023, January 9). Reasons to keep a training journal. *Impact Magazine*, (Inspiration Issue), 90. https://issuu.com/impactmagazinecanada/docs/impact-inspiration-issue-2023-digital/90

Cristiano Ronaldo. (n.d.). *Wikipedia*. https://en.wikipedia.org/w/index.php?title=Cristiano_Ronaldo&oldid=1223310848

De Caux, J. (Director). (2024). *Together: Treble Winners* [Film]. Netflix. https://www.netflix.com/title/81733186

Gao, Z., Chee, C. S., Norjali Wazir, M. R. W., Wang, J., Zheng, X., & Wang, T. (2024). The role of parents in the motivation of young athletes: A systematic review. *Frontiers in Psychology, 14*, 1291711. https://doi.org/10.3389/fpsyg.2023.1291711

Golden State Warriors Stephen (23, December 22). Curry Reads his Pre-Draft Scouting Report [Video]. Facebook. https://www.facebook.com/warriors/videos/227997500248845/

Horowitz, D. (2021, February 10). *How Tom Brady Overcame Adversity To Be a 7x Super Bowl Champion*. Retrieved June 13, 2024, from https://medium.com/@david.horowitz/how-tom-brady-overcame-adversity-to-be-a-7x-super-bowl-champion-3ed98acfea67

Hurford, M. (2021, February 3). *Gratitude journals for sport*. Retrieved May 20, 2024, from https://consummateathlete.com/how-a-gratitude-journal-gets-you-through-athletic-slumps-best-practices/

Inc. (Director). (2017, September 28). *An Olympic gold medalist shares her secret to overcoming negative self-talk*. https://www.youtube.com/watch?v=uBWGfYatMLY

InnerDrive Team. (n.d.). *9 powerful ways Olympians develop resilience | InnerDrive*. https://www.innerdrive.co.uk/blog/9-ways-develop-resilience/

Johnson, S. S. (2021). The science of teamwork. *American Journal of Health Promotion, 35*(5), 730–732. https://doi.org/10.1177/08901171211007955a

Jowett, S., Poczwardowski, A., Denver, U. of, & Arthur. (2007, January). *Understanding the Coach-Athlete Relationship. Researchgate. https://www.researchgate.net/publication/232506356_Understanding_the_Coach-Athlete_Relationship

Karthikeyan, R. (2021, March 13). *"Conscious breathing": Novak Djokovic reveals the secret behind his greatest clutch performances*. EssentiallySports. https://www.essentiallysports.com/tennis-news-atp-conscious-breathing-novak-djokovic-reveals-the-secret-behind-his-greatest-clutch-performances/

Kegelaers, J., & Wylleman, P. (2019). Exploring the coach's role in fostering resilience in elite athletes. *Sport, Exercise, and Performance Psychology, 8*(3), 239–254. https://doi.org/10.1037/spy0000151

Lindsay, R., Spittle, M., & Larkin, P. (2019). The effect of mental imagery on skill performance in sport: A systematic review. *Journal of Science and Medicine in Sport, 22*, S92. https://doi.org/10.1016/j.jsams.2019.08.111

Marks, B. (2013, June 8). *Resilience in sport*. Believe Perform - The UK's Leading Sports Psychology Website. https://members.believeperform.com/resilience-in-sport/

Martínez-Gallego, R., & Molina, D. C. (2019). The influence of non-verbal body language on sport performance in professional tennis. *ITF Coaching and Sport Science Review, 79*(27), 25-27. https://doi.org/10.52383/itfcoaching.v27i79.83

Mazanec, R. (2023, May 19). *What are sports rituals and do they make you play better?* https://www.ncsasports.org/blog/the-benefit-of-sport-rituals

Morehead, J. (2012, June 19). Stanford University's Carol Dweck on the growth mindset and education. *OneDublin.Org*. https://onedublin.org/2012/06/19/stanford-universitys-carol-dweck-on-the-growth-mindset-and-education/

Nicks, P. (Director). (2023). *Stephen Curry: Underrated* [Film]. Apple TV+ Press. https://www.apple.com/tv-pr/originals/stephen-curry-underrated/

Nien, J.-T., Wu, C.-H., Yang, K.-T., Cho, Y.-M., Chu, C.-H., Chang, Y.-K., & Zhou, C. (2020). Mindfulness training enhances endurance performance and executive functions in athletes: An event-related potential study. *Neural Plasticity, 2020*, 1–12. https://doi.org/10.1155/2020/8213710

Nussbaum, A. D., & Dweck, C. S. (2008). Defensiveness versus remediation: Self-theories and modes of self-esteem maintenance. *Personality and Social Psychology Bulletin, 34*(5), 599–612. https://doi.org/10.1177/0146167207312960

Rice, S. M., Treeby, M. S., Olive, L., Saw, A. E., Kountouris, A., Lloyd, M., Macleod, G., Orchard, J. W., Clarke, P., Gwyther, K., & Purcell, R. (2021). Athlete experiences of shame and guilt: Initial psychometric properties of the athletic perceptions of performance scale within junior elite cricketers. *Frontiers in Psychology, 12*, 581914. https://doi.org/10.3389/fpsyg.2021.581914

Sariati, D., Zouhal, H., Hammami, R., Clark, C. C., Nebigh, A., Chtara, M., Hackney, A. C., Souissi, N., Granacher, U., & Ounis, O. B. (2021). Association Between Mental Imagery and Change of Direction Performance in Young Elite Soccer Players of Different Maturity Status. *Frontiers in Psychology, 12:665508*, 1-9. https://doi.org/doi.org/10.3389/fpsyg.2021.665508

Shepherd, Dr. I. (n.d.). *Effective Debriefing—Guided Performance Review*. SimConHealth. https://www.monash.edu/__data/assets/pdf_file/0004/1654222/Effective-Debriefing-with-Guided-Performance-Review-2017.pdf

Shuffler, M. L., Diazgranados, D., Maynard, M. T., & Salas, E. (2018). Developing, sustaining, and maximizing team effectiveness: An integrative, dynamic perspective of team development interventions. *Academy of Management Annals, 12*(2), 688–724. https://doi.org/10.5465/annals.2016.0045

Sporting Bounce (2023, May 2). *Gratitude journals for sport*. Retrieved May 20, 2024, from https://www.sportingbounce.com/blog/gratitude-journals-for-sport

Stephen, F. A., Ermalyn, L. P., Yasmin, M., B., Louise, L. J. D., & Juvenmile, T. B. (2022). A voyage into the visualization of athletic performances: A review. *American Journal of Multidisciplinary Research and Innovation, 1*(3), 105–109. https://doi.org/10.54536/ajmri.v1i3.479

Supporting Champions (Director). (2023, September 26). *Sophia Jowett on the coach-athlete relationship*. https://www.youtube.com/watch?v=AcszyQcDMbs

Taylor, R. D., Collins, D., & Carson, H. J. (2021). The Role of Siblings in Talent Development: Implications for Sports Psychologists and Coaches. *Frontiers in Sports and Active Living, 3*(626327), 1-7. https://doi.org/10.3389/fspor.2021.626327

Tennis TopShots (Director). (2021, November 25). *Rafael Nadal & Roger Federer | the greatest rivalry in tennis—Breakdown of h2h and friendship(P1)*. https://www.youtube.com/watch?v=jrLl-XmqDpA

WatchMojo.com (Director). (2021, April 29). *Top 10 most fascinating sports rituals ever*. https://www.youtube.com/watch?v=dxUwz5DqYAI

Wilson, L. (2015, July 28). Positive self-talk for your athletes. *Coaches Toolbox*. https://www.coachestoolbox.net/mental-toughness/positive-self-talk-for-your-athletes

Yodi, P. (2024, July 8). *David Beckham on Balancing Career and Fatherhood: Exclusive Interview Insights*. Retrieved August 10, 2024, from https://fatherhoodchannel.com/2024/07/08/david-beckham-on-fatherhood/

www.ingramcontent.com/pod-product-compliance
Lightning Source LLC
Chambersburg PA
CBHW072158070526
44585CB00015B/1194